Range Rustlers

Tom Connell is a deputy hired by the Cattlemen's Association to combat rustling on the open range and Clifford Crossley-Hunt, a tough former soldier, works for the Diamond R ranch. Both men arrive in a district where suspected rustlers are lynched and stock thefts are alleged to be excessive. However they soon find that all is not as it is claimed to be.

The matter is further complicated by an unknown gunman who starts killing men from a large local ranch.

Much information is being withheld from Tom and Clifford but they finally forge an alliance which ends in a bloody battle to bring justice to a troubled range.

By the same author

Outlaw Vengeance
Warbonnet Creek
Red Rock Crossing
Killer's Kingdom

Range Rustlers

Greg Mitchell

A Black Horse Western

ROBERT HALE · LONDON

© Greg Mitchell 2008
First published in Great Britain 2008

ISBN 978-0-7090-8567-6

Robert Hale Limited
Clerkenwell House
Clerkenwell Green
London EC1R 0HT

www.halebooks.com

Typeset by
Derek Doyle & Associates, Shaw Heath
Printed and bound in Great Britain by
Antony Rowe Limited, Wiltshire

ONE

The riders from the Double T ranch caught John Murphy in the act. He had a yearling heifer tied down and was branding her with a heated cinch ring held between two sticks. The smell of burning hair and hide hung heavily in the air and the brander was so intent upon his task that he did not notice the five riders who came over the ridge behind him. He had finished his work and was about to set the animal loose when he heard horses galloping toward him. Murphy turned to see Denver Cutler, the Double T foreman, and four cowhands.

The look on Cutler's hatchet face was bad enough but the big Smith & Wesson .44 in his right hand was even more disconcerting. Murphy had no intention of going for his own gun. If he was to get out of this fix he would have to talk his way out.

'Stay right where you are, Murphy.' There was

no friendliness in the foreman's voice although he had known the other for several years. 'You're caught rustling dead to rights.'

'That heifer's a maverick, Denver. No one can lay claim to her. She was missed in the last roundup.'

'But she would have been picked up in the fall. You know that, Murphy. Any mavericks then are divided equally among the members of the Cattlemen's Association.'

'An association that small ranchers are not allowed to join,' Murphy reminded him angrily. 'Who's to say that this heifer was not from one of my own cows?'

'I'm saying it. All mavericks belong to the Association. You're rustling and will be dealt with the same as any other rustler. We're going to string you up.'

'You wouldn't,' Murphy said in disbelief.' Not over one stray heifer, surely? The Association has thousands of head. One maverick makes no difference to them – you couldn't be serious.'

Cutler nodded briefly to the men beside him. 'Rustling is rustling – grab him, boys.'

Murphy reached for his gun but Cutler spurred his horse forward. Its chest hit the man before he could draw his weapon and the impact threw him several feet. Two cowhands came out of their saddles and threw themselves on the fallen man who struggled violently. Murphy's gun eventually cleared the holster but one of his attackers caught his arm and twisted the weapon from his grasp. By this time the other cowhands had joined the fray and by weight of numbers they forced their prisoner to the ground. Though cursing violently Murphy no longer had the strength to resist so many and soon his hands were tied behind his back.

'Get his horse and put him on it,' Cutler ordered, and his lips curled in a grim smile. He was enjoying himself. 'Then we'll find ourselves a suitable tree.'

Things were quiet in the sheriff's office at Lodgepole and Tom Connell had the cylinder out of his Colt .45 as he carefully cleaned the barrel. He had not used the weapon since taking up employment as Sheriff Monty McLeod's deputy but the simple task gave him some means of relieving the boredom. His youthful, tanned face was a study of concentration as he pushed a cleaning brush through the revolver's bore. In his mid-twenties and of average height and build, the dark-haired deputy bore little resemblance to the general idea of a western lawman but he had the qualifications for the job. His was a special position financed by the Cattlemen's Association. He was employed to stop rustling and Connell was soundly experienced in all facets of cattle work. Since his early years he had worked on ranches and several times had travelled up the trail with big herds from Texas. He had also swapped lead with stampeders, bandits and rustlers though he had never considered himself a gunman.

He was just fitting the pin through the revolver frame and cylinder when Jed Roberts, the other deputy came into the office. Roberts was a big man m his mid-thirties and had been in the job for several years. His broad-featured face with its handlebar moustache showed traces of more than one recalcitrant client and he was reckoned a bad man with his fists. 'You'd better get that gun back together and loaded, Tom. There's trouble coming down the street and it could be some of yours.'

'Why's that?' Connell asked, as he began loading the empty cylinder.

'Because there's a few rustlers coming with a wagon and they look serious.'

'Rustlers?'

'They call themselves small ranchers but everyone knows they're behind all the rustling that's going on. There's a whole nest of them in little two-by-four spreads along Alder Creek You'd best get out there and get to know them.'

'Where's Sheriff McLeod?'

'Probably out at Coventry's or one of the other

big spreads. He don't always tell me where he goes.'

Connell arose, slipped the gun back in its holster, put on his hat and strolled out onto the boardwalk just as the wagon and three riders stopped in front of the office.

A small man with a grey spiky beard and a battered black hat, wheeled his bay pony to face the lawman. 'Is McLeod about?' he demanded.

'He isn't. I'm Tom Connell, one of his deputies. Can I help you?'

'I doubt it, sonny, but I'll tell you anyway. I'm Hank Coates. I own the Lazy HC. If you look under this tarpaulin in the wagon you'll see that I'm here about a murder.'

'Do you know who did it?' Connell asked, as he walked to the side of the wagon.

'Some of them fat-gutted coyotes from the Cattlemen's Association, that's who. I've seen their work before.'

Connell lifted the canvas and saw the blackened, distorted face of Murphy. He had died hard at the end of a rope. The deputy had seen such victims before, but had never hoped to see them in his new environment. 'Do you know him?' he asked.

The big, fair-haired man driving the wagon growled, 'It's John Murphy. He was my next-door neighbour.' As he spoke the man produced a crumpled piece of paper. He held it out to

Connell. 'This was stuffed into his shirt pocket.'

The word RUSTLER was printed in pencil in large block letters.

Connell called Roberts. The way the ranchers stiffened at the big deputy's appearance plainly showed that there was no love lost between them. Roberts glanced at the body and then, his curiosity satisfied, he regarded the dead man's friends. 'It was only a matter of time,' he told them. 'Murphy was a known rustler. Looks like somebody finally caught him at it.'

'What are you going to do about it?' Coates demanded.

With obvious satisfaction Roberts pointed to the new deputy. 'This is Tom Connell. He's been specially hired to put an end to the rustling around here. Ask him.'

All eyes turned toward Connell.

'I reckon my first job will be to find out who did this,' he said.

'Then what?' the wagon driver asked.

'I'll arrest them for murder.'

This statement was greeted by snorts of disbelief from the ranchers and a look of alarm from Roberts.

One rancher, a younger man in shotgun chaps said bitterly, 'We've heard all this before. Why should you be different to the other lawmen around here? You're all bought and paid for by the

Cattlemen's Association. You're just another hired gun and have no intention of biting the hand that feeds you.'

'My first job is to uphold the law and I rate murder worse than rustling,' Connell told him quietly. 'But I will need your help. Take Murphy down to the undertaker's and then come back here to the office so I can get some statements from you.'

'We'll do that,' Coates said, as he turned his pony. and led the others away.

'Have you gone crazy?' Roberts demanded, when the others were gone. 'Murphy was caught rustling and got hanged legal. It's always been that way on the cattle ranges. You can't go around arresting everyone who hangs a rustler. Hell, Tom, you'll have the people who are paying your wages in jail.'

'You're dead right. If I find they killed Murphy I'll do my damnedest to convict them. Murder is murder.'

Roberts shook his head like a baffled steer. 'You can't do that. Your job is to stop rustling. You better get a grip on reality or you won't last long around here.'

Half an hour later, after making the funeral arrangements, the ranchers filed into the sheriff's office and Connell took statements from them. George Norton, who had driven the wagon, stated that he had found Murphy hanging from a large pine tree on the open range. Like his neighbours, Norton had a comparatively small spread and ran his cattle on the common range land. He had been checking on his stock when he found the dead man. The tracks indicated that several men were involved in the lynching.

Bill Sutton, the youngest of the group, said that he and his wife saw Denver Cutler and some cowhands riding behind their ranch earlier in the day. By his reckoning these riders would have been in the vicinity when the murder occurred.

It took nearly two hours for Connell to collect the statements and clarify a few points. He could sense the ranchers' impatience and could see by the looks on their faces that they considered the entire process a waste of time. They had departed and the deputy was sorting the statements when Sheriff Monty McLeod lurched in the door.

He was tall and broad-shouldered, about fifty, with thinning red hair. His neat town clothes were those of a man who spent little time in the saddle. The pearl handle of a Colt Lightning showed discreetly under the left side of his coat, but unlike most frontier lawmen he no longer wore a cartridge belt. McLeod liked to think of himself as a cut above the average star-packer. Lately, though, he had been spending most of his time with the big ranchers around the area. From his condition on arrival, he had spent more time sampling their whiskey than discussing the epidemic of rustling.

He leaned against the wall and occasionally blinked like a startled owl as Connell explained what had happened. Roberts stayed in the background and said nothing.

When the deputy had finished talking McLeod said, 'Leave it with me, Tom. I'll handle this. You'd better get out on the range as soon as you can. Jack Coventry said today that he's being robbed blind by rustlers.'

'There's one less now,' Roberts said from the background, as though secretly pleased by Murphy's lynching.

TWO

Clifford Crossley-Hunt was dressed, shaved and ready to eat when the cook on the Diamond R ranch rang the breakfast bell. He stood on the ranch house veranda and surveyed the scene before him, the horses already in the corrals and the cowhands hurrying from the bunkhouse to the kitchen. Some were making last minute adjustments to their clothing or buckling on guns as they went. Though different, the scene vaguely reminded him of similar mornings in various military camps he had seen across the British Empire.

Tall, with aristocratic features, a straight back and neatly trimmed moustache, he retained the bearing of the soldier he once had been. That was before taking up his present employment as a supervisor for Regency Estates, a London-based cattle company with pastoral investments in several countries. It was his first day on the ranch and he was relieved that the long journey by steamer, train and stagecoach, was finally over.

Oliver Jensen, the ranch manager, had greeted him cordially enough, but the visitor knew that, as a representative of the ranch's English owners, he would be regarded with some suspicion. He had not expected what the manager had told him when he arrived; that a rustling problem was threatening the company's profits.

'Breakfast's ready, Captain,' said a quiet voice at his elbow. He turned to see Prudence, the small, middle-aged widow Jensen had employed as a maid, her sharp features set in a worried expression. He had been introduced to her the previous night when he arrived.

'Don't worry about the "Captain", Prudence. I was an army captain not a ship's captain and lost any rank when I left the army. They were probably as pleased to see me go as I was to leave them.'

'Breakfast's ready anyway,' the maid said uncertainly and walked away.

Crossley-Hunt found Jensen waiting for him and impatiently eyeing the ham and eggs on his plate. The manager was a thin man of middle age with a habitually worried expression. He greeted the newcomer, made a brief enquiry about how well he had slept and, with little apparent interest in replies, attacked his breakfast. His hunger partially satisfied, he then questioned the visitor as to his plans.

'I want to have a ride around the range and see the situation. The company was unaware that cattle-stealing was such a problem,' Crossley-Hunt told him. 'We need to know the extent of it and what steps are needed to counteract it.'

The last thing Jensen wanted was to play nurse-maid to some English dude, specially one who might accidentally discover too much. The more time the company man spent on the open range, the less chance he had of uncovering the manager's secret dealings. 'I can get our foreman Ed Adams to tell you all that. I'm sure you don't want to be riding all over the place, but the more time you spend on the open range the better you will appreciate conditions here. I suppose you can ride.'

'I can ride and I enjoy it. As you know, my work entails first-hand reports to the Regency Estates' directors. I know that you make monthly reports, but they take a long time to reach London and circumstances are often changed by the time they do. I am sure, too, that we do not fully understand the conditions that apply here. It might save you a lot of writing if I have a better idea of the situation.'

'Suit yourself,' Jensen said, but he did not sound pleased. He rang a small bell on the table and Prudence appeared. 'Go to Ed and tell him to saddle a quiet horse for Mr Crossways-Hunt.'

*

Connell could scarcely believe his eyes when the rider unexpectedly rode into his camp. The last person he expected to see was a pretty girl with the light-brown hair who looked a picture aboard a smart grey pony. It was obvious from the way that she checked her mount as she emerged from the willows bordering the creek that the girl had not expected to meet anyone either.

The deputy hastily dropped the map he was studying and raised his hat. 'Howdy,' he said as he rose to his feet.

The girl smiled and returned his greeting. Pointing to the map he had dropped, she observed, 'You look like you might be lost.'

'Not really – I'm just getting to know the country a bit. I expect to be working around here for a while.'

A glint of suspicion showed in those green eyes. 'Oh – what ranch?'

Connell was not one to beat about the bush. He would have preferred to remain undiscovered for a couple of days but could see no point in telling lies. 'I guess you could say that I'll be on all the ranches eventually. I'm Tom Connell, a deputy hired to stop this rustling that has folks so worried.'

The friendly smile disappeared. 'Only certain

17

folks are worried about rustling. Others say it's not happening. My folks own the C 2 Bar and we don't have any trouble – leastways not from rustlers. You won't find any rustlers around here, but if you wanted to be useful, you could be looking for the men who murdered John Murphy.'

'Sheriff McLeod's looking into that.'

A flush of anger appeared on the girl's face. 'The only thing he looks into is the mirror behind the bar in Mason's saloon. He has not caught one of those killers yet.'

Connell was surprised. 'Do you mean there has been more than one murder?'

'This was the second such killing. Didn't McLeod tell you that?'

'No he didn't. Who do you think is behind it?'

'Your employers, the Cattlemen's Association – who else? Some of them only own a few acres but they are crowding out the free range with big herds that otherwise they could not feed. They want to push us smaller ranchers off so they can increase their herds even more. That English company that owns the Diamond R, is a good example. They are running something like five thousand head. Coventry's Wineglass brand is running nearly as many. Raymond's Double T has thousands of head too.'

'And how many does your ranch own – Miss. . . ?'

18

'I'm Mary Coulter. We have around four hundred head on the open range. Some of our neighbours are much the same. It is not our herds that are eating out the free grass – and we don't steal cattle.'

'I'm glad to hear that, Miss Coulter, because if that is the case you need not worry about me.'

'Then why are you skulking around here?' she demanded suspiciously.

With difficulty Connell kept his anger in check. 'I'm not skulking anywhere. I could make my base at one of the ranches, but then my impartiality would be questioned by one side or the other. I'm not taking sides in any disputes over grass. I am here to investigate claims of rustling and to stop any further killing if I can. Over the next few days I'll be calling at most of the ranches and I'll be out on the open range too. You can tell your friends that I'll be around.'

'I intend to,' the girl snapped. Then she wheeled her pony about and cantered back the way she had come.

An hour later Connell was guiding his chestnut horse around a cow track on a steep hill. His bay pack horse followed obediently without needing to be led. Down the slope from the track he saw a weathered carcass on a section of flat ground beside a small creek. Here's as good a place as any to start, he told himself, and turned the chestnut down the slope.

The dead steer looked strangely shrunken and obviously had been lying there for some weeks, but Connell had seen such sights before. The skin had partially collapsed and he knew why: there was no carcass underneath. Someone had killed the steer, butchered it on the hide but left the head and lower legs attached to the skin. A few strategically placed sticks under the hide held it up enough to give the appearance of a body underneath, as though the animal had died of natural causes and rotted away. The ruse might have worked if scavenging animals had not knocked away some of the props leaving the supposed carcass looking strangely flat. The hide was half rotted, but the deputy could discern that it bore the Double T brand. A bullet hole in the skull showed where the animal had been shot. He had seen such work before. These slaughterings were never part of large-scale rustling operations and could be either the work of small settlers down on their luck, or big ranchers too mean to kill their own stock for beef. Even people from towns had been known to come out, slaughter a steer and carry the meat away in a wagon. Although in this case a wagon could not have negotiated the rough country. The meat would have been packed out.

Some small-scale rustling was inevitable but, to Connell's mind, the days of large numbers of stock being run off were over. Branded cattle were hard to sell illegally and altering brands involved holding large numbers of stock in areas where they might be discovered. With a walking speed of about two miles per hour, it would take a long time to shift stolen stock out of a particular area. Though brands could be changed, ranch cattle were also ear-marked and altering these marks was difficult.

The deputy remounted his horse and continued his patrol. If rustling was occurring on a large-scale, he was sure that he would find signs.

He knew that the large ranchers never had an exact count of their stock and simply multiplied their annual brandings by three. If the calf crop was noticeably down they might suspect a rustling problem, but it was difficult to be sure. Connell knew that he had many more enquiries to make before he would have the full picture.

THREE

Crossley-Hunt had seen variations of the same situation many times before. The cowhands were trying him out. He had acquired a wide-brimmed hat and replaced his tie with a bandanna but his eastern riding breeches and long shiny boots still marked him as a dude.

Ed Adams had first arrived with a sleepy, fat pinto horse whose scarred knees showed that he was not very good on his legs. It also demonstrated the foreman's contempt for the visitor's riding ability. The company man was singularly unimpressed and promptly told him to select something better and, if he could not, he was to surrender his own mount. After all, the company owned it. A short while later the foreman reappeared with a smart-looking bay gelding and a few grinning cowhands riding behind.

Crossley-Hunt knew that Adams would not risk

being fired by giving him an unrideable horse but he was sure that the animal they brought him would test out his ability. It would be the sort of horse that a competent cowhand was expected to ride. As though unsuspecting, he checked the length of his stirrups, the tightness of the cinch, and casually stepped aboard. The bay walked a couple of paces, then with no warning, dropped its head and launched itself skywards. It hit the ground and came back under him, a hard buck to ride at any time, but the Englishman was still in the saddle. The animal only knew one trick and, when its best effort failed, it gave a couple more crow hops before lifting its head and walking off.

'If you fellows think this horse could buck,' he told the obviously disappointed spectators, 'you should try riding some of the Australian Waler remounts we had in India, and we had only Nolan military saddles. Game time is over now but there is one more thing: my name is Crossley-Hunt and anyone who calls me Crossways or Crosscut or some other variation will soon be looking for another job when he picks himself out of the dirt.' He could see that the message was not lost on Adams and continued, 'Now I want to have a look around the range. I only need Mr Adams and possibly one other man, so the rest of you might as well go back to what you are supposed to be doing.'

They rode for a couple of hours, first around the ranch where a few stud animals and horses were kept. Adams volunteered no information and replied only when questioned directly. The company man noted that fences, corrals and sheds were in good order and that the animals were in good condition. Finally the trio rode out on the open range where most of their stock lived between roundups and sales.

Stock of many different breeds and brands grazed together but Crossley-Hunt could not help noticing that a large number wore the Double T on the left hip and had a T-shaped piece clipped from the right ear. He remarked to Adams,' The Double T seems to be running a considerable number of stock. How would they know that they are losing cattle to rustlers?'

'They know – we all know,' the foreman replied vaguely. 'Rustling is one hell of a problem.'

It was the cowhand riding with them who first drew attention to the fresh horse tracks. 'Someone's around,' he said quietly. 'Maybe he's up to no good.'

'He could also be someone checking on stock, the same as we are,' Crossley-Hunt suggested. 'Let's not jump to conclusions.'

Adams reined in his horse and pointed. The rider in the distance might not have been noticed against the dark green pines if it had not been for the grey horse. 'Someone over there,' the foreman said. 'Do we go after him? He has a long start on us.'

Crossley-Hunt looked in a slightly different direction and saw two saddled horses at a low point on the valley floor. 'Let's see what's happening with those horses first.'

Connell watched the riders approach. Two were obviously cattlemen, but the leading rider looked different. His gleaming, black boots advertised that he had not been in too many dusty corrals. When the stranger called, 'Hello there,' he knew that he was not looking at a rustler.

Connell walked over to the trio. 'Howdy,' he greeted. 'I'm Tom Connell. It's a good day for a ride, but you men look like you're on business. What ranch are you from?'

After the others introduced themselves, Adams said that Connell's name sounded familiar Then he remembered. 'You're the new special deputy hired to keep an eye on rustlers. Have you seen any yet?'

'Can't say I have but there's a sign of them just over here. It is small-scale stuff and it's not recent. This steer has been killed for meat. Unfortunately it doesn't tell us much about who butchered this animal and the way things are there would be no shortage of suspects. The prevailing view on the open range is that a man chokes if he eats his own beef. Big ranchers and small ranchers have all been guilty of this. All we can assume is that the butcher was not from the Double T because it would be too far to pack home the beef and there would be no need to conceal what they had done.'

Adams said angrily, 'It wasn't anyone from the Diamond R. We don't touch other ranches' cows. We kill our own beef.'

'Glad to hear it,' Connell observed.

Crossley-Hunt suggested that the deputy should return to the ranch with them and discuss matters with Oliver Jensen, the manager. As this was something he had intended to do anyway, it suited Connell's plans to accept the invitation.

'We saw a rider on a grey horse not far from here,' Crossley-Hunt told him. 'He disappeared over a hill before we could get a good look at him.'

The deputy's only comment was, 'It's open range. That rider probably had as much right to be here as anyone else. Uncle Sam owns this country, not those who are running cattle on it.' He saw no point in involving Mary Coulter unnecessarily.

While riding back to the ranch, he questioned his companions about the rustling problem. As a visitor, Crossley-Smith did not know much so Adams did most of the talking. The foreman's answers seemed to be coming from a carefully prepared script with many general claims but few specific details. Satisfied that he was getting nowhere, Connell allowed the talk to swing around to cattle.

The Diamond R had recently imported eight young Black Angus bulls from Scotland in an attempt to improve the quality of their mixed-breed herd. Adams made no secret of his dislike for the new strain. He disliked muley cattle on the grounds that they had no defence against predators and the new bulls were not the long, low animals he had been expecting. In his opinion they were rather ordinary.

Crossley-Smith mentioned that he had seen a few in Kansas as he travelled west. The breed was comparatively new in the United States but was gaining popularity. One advantage was that when crossed with other breeds, they produced all-black calves that looked to be good beef types.

'That may be,' Connell observed, 'but I knew a Scot who came over with one of the first shipments in 'seventy-three. He said that these Angus cattle, if crossed with dairy breeds—'

Any further comment ceased when the foreman pointed to the distant ranch house. 'There's a few horses tied outside. Looks like we have visitors. It ain't usual to have so many people calling at once. I reckon something's wrong.'

'We will soon find out,' said Crossley-Hunt.

FOUR

The visitors turned out to be Joe Raymond, owner of the Double T and a couple of his cowhands. The rancher was short but broad-shouldered with a neatly trimmed grey beard and wore wire-framed spectacles. His age was hard to guess but he moved like a comparatively young man. When introduced to Connell, he muttered, 'You're just the one I need. My foreman, Denver Cutler was murdered this morning. I'm getting some men together to go after his killer.'

'Do you know who killed him?' Connell asked.

The rancher looked at him as though he was a backward child. 'It was rustlers, sonny, the same ones behind all the trouble here. He just walked out of the bunkhouse door this morning and someone put a rifle bullet through his heart – killed him stone dead.'

'Any idea why he was shot?' Connell enquired.

Raymond looked vaguely uncomfortable and glanced at Jensen before replying, 'No – no idea at all.'

The answer did not ring true and the deputy could see that some of the others seemed uneasy about the reply. Jensen looked about uncomfortably. Adams looked as though he was about to say something but thought better of it.

'This wouldn't have anything to do with the Murphy lynching?' Connell persisted.

'Of course not.' The denial came a little too quickly.

'Just where were you intending to start looking for the killer?'

'Where he came from, one of those little two-by-four outfits along Alder Creek. Now I suggest that you stop asking questions and do what we're paying you to do.'

'I'll do that,' Connell said quietly, 'just as soon as you people give me enough information so that I know where to start looking. Has Sheriff McLeod been advised?'

'I sent a man to tell him,' Raymond growled. 'Now let's get moving.'

Jensen told his foreman. 'Take a couple of the boys and go with them.'

'Go where?' the deputy demanded.

'Where else? To Alder Creek to clear out that nest of murdering rustlers once and for all.'

'I'll go with you,' Crossley-Hunt announced. 'Just wait while I get my revolver from my room.'

Connell disapproved of a vengeful posse riding around the countryside, but figured that enquiries had to start somewhere and Alder Creek would have to be looked at anyway. Hoping to be a steadying influence, he decided to ride with the group and arranged to leave his pack horse and pack at the ranch. He was unloading the animal when, to his annoyance, the posse rode away without him. But he was not the only one left behind.

Crossley-Hunt appeared on the veranda wearing a military-style gunbelt. He looked in dismay at the rapidly diminishing dust cloud in the distance. Connell intercepted him as he was running to where he had left his horse. 'Take your time,' he told him. 'They'll be easy to track.'

'They might at least have waited, 'specially Adams and the Diamond R men. They're not working for the Double T.'

Connell checked the cinches on his saddle and mounted. 'It seems that for some reason they don't want you and me around and that in itself is a bit of a worry. It's not just impatience; I suspect they are planning something illegal so I'm following them anyway. Would you care to join me?'

'Why not? It's a good day for a ride.'

Oliver Jensen watched the pair ride away with a sense of relief The Englishman's presence was a worry. The longer he spent away from the ranch, the safer the manager felt. How convenient it would be if Crossley-Hunt was to be shot by the rustlers or suffer some other fatal accident.

Mary Coulter could hardly wait to tell her parents that a sheriff's deputy was in the area.

Ben Coulter with an aching back and a mouth-ful of horseshoe nails was in no position to comment as he started nailing the final shoe on a fractious black mare. He listened with growing unease as Mary told him of the new deputy.

Coulter continued driving and clenching down the nails. 'Go and tell your mother and find out where your brother is. I reckon trouble's on the way. I'll be along soon as I finish here. Some of these special deputies are only hired killers brought in by the big ranchers. I don't want you or Bob out on the range with one of them murdering coyotes about.'

FIVE

Bob Coulter steered his grulla pony around the places where the cattle were lying up in the shade. Though only seventeen, he had spent most of his life among cattle and knew better than to disturb them when they were resting out of the noonday heat and chewing their cuds. He had been checking on his father's cattle and keeping an eye out for any young stock that might have been missed in the spring roundup or had been born since then. It was important that they still followed Coulter cows because if they were weaned, the big ranchers were likely to claim them as mavericks at the fall roundup. Though the family cattle were mixed with those of other ranches and scattered over miles of range, he saw no evidence that any C2 Bar calves had been missed in the spring.

His pony gave the first sign of danger and threw up its head as it heard the beat of approaching hoofs. The boy felt uneasy as he remembered the lynch mob that some claimed was stalking the range. Though his conscience was clear, Bob knew that he could be a target because of his father's small-rancher status. He grew increasingly nervous and tried to tell himself that it was only some cowhands in a hurry, but something in his mind was whispering danger. The sounds grew louder and then, as suddenly as a war party of raiding Sioux, a group of riders burst over the low hill to his left. Also like Indian raiders, the riders whooped in triumph when they sighted him and increased their pace. The boy had seen enough. He wheeled his pony about and rode hard for home. The horsemen yelled and followed, the thrill of the chase overcoming natural caution on the rough ground. One of the pursuers even fired an ineffective shot which immediately dispelled Bob's doubts as to any peaceful intentions.

The boy had less than a hundred yards start and rode hard to increase his gain. The closer his enemies came, the greater were his chances of being hit by a bullet. He was more than a mile from the back boundary of their ranch and would have to nurse his pony carefully if he hoped to reach it. The grulla had been a good horse but now was past its best. Although lightly weighted, the rough ground and the pace would soon begin to take their toll.

Raymond and Adams had lived long enough to know that riding hard through such country was a good way to get hurt so they slowed their pace and allowed the younger, more reckless cowhands to keep up the pursuit. They could keep the others in sight with less risk to themselves.

Connell and Crossley-Hunt were also in the vicinity. They had taken a fairly leisurely pace until they heard that first shot. Spurring their horses up a nearby ridge, they looked about. A tiny dust cloud showed the location of the quarry and the hunters not far behind. The latter were stretched out in a long line depending upon the speed of their horses and the nerve of their riders.

Connell pointed ahead. 'We can take a couple of short cuts by staying on the ridge line.'

Crossley-Hunt slightly shortened his reins, 'Lead on.'

Bob's pony was tiring. It was covered in foaming sweat and its head was lowering as it neared the end of its endurance. The boy had tried every trick he knew to spare his mount but the pursuers were gradually closing the gap. A glance over his shoulder showed that they would soon be in revolver range.

Then the pony fell. There was no stumbling or warning of any kind. It just crashed to the earth and threw its rider out ahead of it. The boy hit the ground, rolled and came up on his feet. Defiantly he drew his gun. He had no intention of finishing up like John Murphy. The gun was an old Navy Colt loaded with paper cartridges and he would only have five shots. For safety's sake he had the hammer resting on an empty chamber.

The speed of his reaction took the foremost rider by surprise and when he saw himself looking down the Colt's bore, he swung his mount away. The slight delay gave Bob the chance to take refuge in a shallow ditch.

A cowhand on a flashy pinto horse was next on the scene. He snapped a shot at the boy but missed. Bob fired back and had the satisfaction of seeing the man drop his gun and clutch at the saddle horn.

'Get back!' one of the hunters shouted urgently and set the example by spurring his mount out of pistol range. Seeing the sense in his action the others followed. They could have ridden over their quarry, but it was likely to cost them lives. Bob was on foot with nowhere to go and it would be much easier and far safer to kill him from long range with a rifle.

The retreating men almost collided with Raymond and Adams in their haste to get out of pistol range. The boss of the Diamond R snorted in derision. 'A fine bunch you are. Running from a kid with an old cap-and-ball pistol.'

'He shot Luke,' one cowhand told him.

Adams swore as the wounded man crumpled and fell from his saddle. He did not need to lose one of their men with a company representative visiting the ranch. 'Andy,' he snapped, 'see what you can do for Luke. The rest of you blow that murdering little sonofabitch to hell.'

Just then Crossley-Smith and the deputy galloped up to join them. Raymond muttered angrily. This was not the time for witnesses.

'What's going on here?' Connell demanded.

'That kid over there shot one of our men,' Adams growled. 'Stay out of this.'

'I saw what happened. Why were you chasing him? In that kid's position I would have done the same thing.'

'He's a rustler,' Raymond announced. 'He's one of the Coulters.'

Crossley-Hunt reined in his horse opposite the rancher. 'I assume you have proof that the boy was rustling, Mr Raymond. What exactly was he doing? Did you see him rustling stock?'

'Er – not this time. But he took off as soon as he saw us.'

The Englishman looked hard at him. 'Under the circumstances, I think he showed good sense.' Then he turned to Adams. 'Forget about the boy. See what you can do for that wounded man.'

The foreman flushed angrily and retorted, 'You can't give me orders. Jensen's my boss. I don't take orders from some dude whose mother wasn't even sure of his father's name and could only name the two most likely suspects.'

Crossley-Hunt ignored the insult. 'You will take orders from me and so will Jensen. 1 am a special inspector for Regency Estates and I have the authority to fire you. As it is, I am resisting the urge to drag you off that horse and give you a lesson in manners.'

Noting the closed flap on the Englishman's holster, Adams moved his right hand over his gun butt. 'Just try it.'

The double click of a gun being cocked caught the foreman's attention. He looked to see Connell's Colt trained on him.

'I'll shoot you if you try to draw that gun,' the deputy announced. 'There's been too much shooting around here today, but I'll make an exception in your case if you try anything. If you and Mr Crossley-Hunt want to settle your differences with your fists, that's fine with me. Otherwise, if you want to keep your job, you'll do as he says.'

A startled oath from Raymond quickly defused the situation. The others followed the direction of his gaze and saw three horsemen, each carrying a rifle, halted on a ridge above them.

'It's Coulter and Sutton and Norton's there too,' a cowhand said. 'Looks like they mean business.'

Connell thought quickly. The situation was getting more volatile by the minute. 'Stay here and nobody start shooting.'

He urged his horse forward and rode slowly toward Bob Coulter.

The boy saw him coming and began sighting along his gun barrel. The deputy raised his right hand high to show that he was not reaching for a gun. Bob watched nervously and kept his gun trained on the approaching rider's shirt front. 'Don't come any closer,' he shouted.

Connell halted his mount about five yards away. 'You won't need that gun,' the deputy told him. 'You're not in any trouble with the law. My name's Tom Connell. I'm a sheriff's deputy. If you want to catch your pony and go, I'll make sure no one bothers you.'

'You're one of McLeod's men. I can't trust you any more than I'd trust those others.'

'Your pa and a couple of your neighbours have their rifles trained on me right now. If I make one wrong move they'll shoot me quick.'

'You're just trying to make me look behind so you'll be able to draw your gun. I ought to shoot you right now.'

'Don't do anything rash.' Connell stood in his stirrups and shouted, 'Coulter.'

'What do you want?' a voice replied.

The boy's relief was clearly visible but he still

eyed the deputy nervously.

'Your boy is going to catch his pony and ride up to you. I'll make sure he's not harmed.'

'He better not be,' Coulter shouted back. 'There's three rifles trained on you.'

Connell walked his horse beside Bob to screen him from Raymond and the others while he caught the grulla. 'You shot a man back there and, for the record, I need to know what happened. I arrived on the scene a bit late but I saw them chasing you. Why was that?'

'I was checking on our cattle when that bunch of riders came charging over a hill after me. Two small ranchers have been lynched so far and I don't intend to be the third.'

'That's fair enough. When you get home, tell your folks that I'll be riding around out here for a while. I'll probably call on them sometime over the next few days.'

Bob caught his pony, checked it over for injuries and finding none, mounted it. 'Thanks,' he called back as he rode away.

The deputy returned to the others. Raymond was far from happy and Adams and Crossley-Hunt were both glaring at each other. The wounded man was stretched out on the ground. The bullet had glanced off a rib and lodged in his upper arm leaving painful but not life-threatening wounds. The country was too rough for a wheeled vehicle and though it would be painful, the injured man would be forced to ride out.

While all attention was on the wounded man, Adams quietly mounted his horse and slipped away.

SIX

Raymond was in a foul mood as he steered his horse toward the Double T. His hunt for rustlers had been frustrated and one of his men wounded. Interference by Connell had broken up the posse and the small ranchers were aware of their presence. The vital element of surprise was gone. Further incursions into the Alder Creek area were likely to be dangerous.

Luther Schultz, the man chosen to replace Cutler as foreman, was riding at his side. Schultz might not have been as smart as Cutler but he was just as hard, an uncompromising, utterly ruthless man. He shared the same hatred of rustlers as Raymond and Cutler had.

'Too bad that Connell turned up when he did,' the new foreman muttered. 'We would have really hurt those rustlers if we had strung up Bob Coulter. The Coulters are the brains behind those thieving ranchers.'

In a pine thicket not far ahead, a young, olive-skinned man checked the sights on his Winchester. He had chosen his ambush site well, A screen of trees concealed him from his intended victims and a deep arroyo at the side of the trail would stop any direct pursuit. He raised his rifle and smiled to himself as Schultz rode into his sights. Taking a deep breath, he squeezed the trigger. The rifle kicked solidly against his shoulder and the thump of a bullet striking flesh came back to the shooter's ears.

The heavy lead slug hit Schultz just above his gunbelt, knocking him halfway from his saddle and doubling him up as it ploughed through his body like a hot iron. Raymond's horse reacted before its rider and jumped sideways. The riders behind scattered and the stricken man slid gasping to the ground as his mount shied.

The unseen gunman fired again and Ben Richmond, another of the cowhands, yelped in alarm as a bullet cut a piece from his ear.

All was confusion. Men were yelling and horses plunging at the frantic directions of their riders.

Raymond jumped from his saddle, drew a carbine from its scabbard and sheltered behind his prancing horse as best he could. His men did likewise, dodging among the startled horses and trying to keep from being trampled.

'He's across the arroyo in the pines,' a cowhand shouted. 'I saw gunsmoke over there.'

'We can't get at him if he is,' Raymond said. Then, raising his voice, he called, 'Fire into those pines.'

Rifle fire tore through the dark green trees but the shooter had already gone.

Crossley-Hunt watched the small ranchers and then the Double T men depart. It was then that he missed the foreman. 'Where's Adams?' he asked.

'He ain't here,' a man replied with studied insolence.

Very calmly, the company man told him, 'You won't be here much longer either if you don't tell me when he left and where he was going. Now try another answer.'

His bluff called, the cowhand mumbled, 'He left about five minutes ago. Looked like he was going back to the ranch – didn't say nothing to nobody.'

Suspecting that Adams had gone running to Jensen, Crossley-Hunt turned his horse's head and said to Connell. 'I'm going back to the ranch. Are you coming?'

'I reckon I will,' the deputy replied. 'I have to pick up my pack horse and pack.'

'Why not stay at the Double T tonight?'

'I'm tempted but my place is out on the range and I can't afford to have people think that I'm

43

taking sides.'

The ride back was uneventful until they passed the fenced pasture where the stud bulls were kept. Being unfamiliar with the breed, Connell rode over to the fence for a closer look. He found himself agreeing with Adams that that the new bulls looked fairly ordinary and he could not see any value in importing such animals. The closest bull stared at him curiously. He saw its shiny black coat and the only colour otherwise was a slight orange tinge inside the ears. Vaguely he recalled his conversation with the Scottish herdsman. There was something negative about those little patches of colour but he could not recall exactly what it was. 'Do you know much about that breed?' he asked Crossley-Hunt.

The Englishman shook his head. 'I'm more of a business manager than a cattle specialist but I do know that these Black Angus cattle produce very good beef.'

Connell did not sound convinced. 'Maybe you people and us have different ideas about what is good beef but I don't reckon those critters are carrying as much beef as some range bulls I've seen.'

When they reached the corrals, the deputy collected his pack horse and commenced loading his pack saddle again. He preferred to remain outside while Jensen and Crossley-Hunt discussed the Double T foreman's insubordination. He saw no sign of Adams himself but figured that he would be in the ranch house with his boss. When he was ready to leave he led his horses over to the main house. A small worried-looking woman with grey-streaked hair was sweeping the veranda. The sound of loud, agitated voices was drifting from the house.

Deeming it best not to interrupt, Connell halted at the steps and said to the woman, 'Sounds like this isn't a good time to horn in on the discussion, Ma'am. Would you mind telling any survivors that Deputy Connell is grateful for them looking after his horse and that he'll see them later.'

Prudence stopped her sweeping. 'I'll do that,' she promised.

Jensen looked out the window in time to see the deputy riding away. He turned again to Crossley-Hunt. 'I know that Ed got out of line but he was doing his best to protect the company's interests. This rustling has been knocking down our stock numbers and we're all sick of it. He has been an important factor in the smooth running of this place so I'm relieved that you have agreed to him staying on.'

Crossley-Hunt sat back in his chair. 'He nearly had us involved in a murder today, Mr Jensen. He keeps his job only if he sticks to ranch work and leaves the apprehension of rustlers to the relevant authorities. I want that clearly understood.'

The rancher produced a pipe and began to stuff it with tobacco. 'That's understood. What would you like to do tomorrow?'

'I might take a ride over and see some of those small ranchers and hear their side of the story.'

'You won't get much from them. Jack Coventry's coming over tomorrow from the Wineglass. He'll be more informative.'

'I'll get around to him before I leave,' the company man said.

A little too eagerly Jensen asked 'When will that be?'

'When I get a good idea of the true situation around here. The company went to a lot of expense to send me here and I need to provide a full report backed up by relevant facts and figures.'

The man crouched over a small fire in a deep coulee where the flames would be hard to see. In the flickering light he studied a crumpled piece of paper he had taken from his pocket. It was a list of five names. The topmost name of Denver Cutler had already been crossed off. A smile appeared on the man's face as he drew a pencil line through the name of Schultz. He was gut shot and would die in great pain. Only three more names to go.

SEVEN

Next day Connell found more evidence of rustling. The steer had been killed and butchered on the hide leaving the head legs and bones behind. The slaughter was typical of someone in a hurry who had just carved the meat off the bones instead of talking whole quarters. Once more the method of slaughter indicated a small-time rustler. In this case though, the rustler had taken the hide and the deputy was a bit puzzled by that. There were no brands on fresh beef but a branded hide could be incriminating.

He found long trails of dried manure in places which indicated that the cattle were being driven, but that was no indicator of illegal activity. They seemed to be from cattle moving down from the higher slopes to the lower, more open country where the scattered stock would be gathered at round-up time. Had the signs been more recent the situation would have been different. For hours Connell criss-crossed the open range looking for signs of branding fires or hidden corrals in box canyons. He had been in areas where rustling had been rife and knew the signs of such activities, but saw nothing to indicate that the problem was widespread. Perhaps, he told himself, he had not seen enough country yet to make an informed judgement. One thing was certain; the range was heavily stocked.

Crossley-Hunt had finished breakfast and was endeavouring to strike up a conversation with Prudence on the ranch-house veranda. The maid, however, seemed too shy to talk and only replied in monosyllables. The company man knew from experience that those engaged in menial tasks had often acquired more knowledge about a venture's operations than was realized by the employers. But the conversation never really got started.

They heard the beating hoofs shortly before a rider on a foam-covered horse burst into view from around a clump of pines near the front gate. The rider saw them and halted his mount in front of the house. 'Where's Jensen?' he demanded. 'I have a message for him from Joe Raymond.'

The ranch manager had heard the messenger arrive and strode out onto the veranda. 'What's the trouble?' he demanded.

'Schultz got shot yesterday and died last night. Sheriff McLeod is raising a posse to go looking for the killer. If you're coming you'd better start getting your men together. Jack Coventry is bringing a few hands too. Raymond reckons there'll never be a better chance to clear out those rustlers. The posse's meeting on that grassy flat near the crossing at Big Squaw Creek.'

Jensen looked puzzled. 'Who in the hell is Schultz?'

'He rode for the Double T. Rustlers ambushed our men last night and Schultz got hisself gut shot. The Coulter kid shot another one of our hands, too. We've had two men shot in one day.'

'I'll be with you,' Jensen said. 'Prudence !' he bellowed over his shoulder.

'I'm here Mr Jensen,' the maid said quietly.

'Find Ed. Tell him to get the hands saddled up and ready to ride.' Seeing Crossley-Hunt standing nearby, the ranch manager said, 'Do you fancy a bit of excitement, Clifford?'

'No, thank you, Oliver,' the company man said. 'I'll leave the legal work to the sheriff. If you will leave out the account books and stock records I'll catch up with some paperwork while you are gone.'

Though pretending to be joking, Jensen asked, 'You ain't scared you might get shot, are you?'

'Not particularly. I've been fired upon so often

49

that I have become almost used to it, but I am paid to be here, not out chasing murderers. You are also paid to be here, but I realize that you might have to perform some civic duties as well. I have no such excuse. I'll see you when you get back.'

Sheriff McLeod sat back in the shade of a cottonwood tree and took a furtive swig from the flask carried his in his coat pocket. He smiled a little at the spectacle of the diminutive Jack Coventry dismounting from his very tall black horse by taking both feet from the stirrups and sliding off like an Eastern dude. He told himself that one day a cantankerous horse might kick some sense into the man whose vanity forced him to ride only the tallest horses to cover his lack of height. The big lawman chuckled and said, 'You need to keep riding those old plugs, Jack, if you keep getting off in such a damn fool way. A horse with a bit of life in it could cow kick you into the middle of next week.'

Coventry ignored the jibe, hitched up his studded gunbelt and looked around. 'Who are we waiting for, Monty?'

'Ollie Jensen and a couple of his hands will be along soon. Joe Raymond is over there under those trees. Just sit here a while and I'll tell you what's going on and how we need to handle this. I picked up Chico after I heard the news and I'll use him to run the killer's tracks. He ain't the prettiest 'breed I've seen but he sure knows how to track a man.'

The rancher looked over to where a swarthy, lean man in buckskins was holding a ribby little roan mustang. The tracker was quietly smoking a cigarette as he saw the posse assembling. He was a loner who displayed no particulr regard for his fellow humans, a seemingly friendless man whose sole redeeming feature appeared to be his tracking ability.

Raymond ambled across to join the sheriff and Coventry. He was troubled by a thought that kept occurrng. While some of his men had reasoned that Schultz had been in the wrong place at the wrong time, he had other suspicions. After checking to be sure that he was not overheard, he said quietly to McLeod, 'I think that whoever shot Schultz knew exactly who he was aiming for. Cutler and Schultz were in the party that strung up John Murphy. This is some sort of revenge killing. I reckon someone knows who was involved and, if I'm right, Lonsdale, Quinn and Hutchins could be next.'

'Well, don't expect me to know,' the sheriff told him. 'I didn't know for sure who was invloved until you just told me and I didn't want to know. If you are right, someone on the Double T has been talking, or else the hanging was seen by one of the small ranchers who knew the men concerned.'

The arrival of Jensen and his men stopped further discussion. The others quickly mounted although there was a slight delay while Coventry found a low spot to stand his horse so that his foot could reach the stirrup enabling him to mount.

Chico was ready when McLeod trotted his horse over to him and said, 'Find that killer for me, Chico.'

EIGHT

Connell saw the chimney smoke rising above a screen of pines and heard the sound of someone chopping wood. Then he encountered a track running into the trees and, when he followed it, he came to a gate. A C2 Bar burned into the gatepost told him that he was entering Coulter's ranch.

The rancher's dogs were barking long before the deputy came into view. When he emerged from the trees he saw a roomy, neat cabin with a large vegetable garden beside it and a plentiful supply of split wood. There was washing on the line but no sign of the axeman he had heard as he approached He saw some movement behind the window curtains beside the door and noticed that the latter was very slightly ajar. He stopped his horse, stood in the stirrups and called, 'Anyone home?'

The door opened and Coulter emerged with no

welcome on his face and a shotgun in his hands. 'What do you want?'

'We met yesterday, Mr Coulter. 1 was wondering if you could give me a bit of information. I'll be calling at all the ranches in the area.'

'You're wasting your time, Connell. I ain't gonna give you anything that you'll use against me or my neighbours later.'

'I'm not here asking you to give away secrets. l'm here to investigate what is claimed to be an outbreak of rustling and I haven't been able to find any evidence of such a great outbreak. I would like your ideas about the situation.'

'They are the same as I said all along: there never was any rustling,' Coulter growled. 'It's a story cooked up by the big ranchers to give them an excuse to force out the rest of us.'

'There's some rustling; I've seen signs of it. There's always a bit in open-range country, but that's nothing. Have you ever lost any cattle or has your calf crop been unexpectedly down?'

'Can't say for sure that I have,' the rancher replied. 'But with cattle the unexpected often happens. I ain't saying though that I have more calves than cows in a given year, if that's what you're driving at.'

'It's not. But we do need to talk.'

Coulter's suspicions had waned slightly and he finally invited the deputy to dismount and come inside. Mary and Bob Coulter just had time to put away the guns with which they were covering their father before the visitor entered the house. Shirley Coulter, their mother, greeted Connell at the door and then hurried to the kitchen to prepare a pot of coffee.

The rancher indicated a chair near the front window. 'Take a seat there and let's hear what you have to say.'

Crossley-Hunt put aside the ranch books. He hated book work at the best of times but knew that a certain amount was necessary. As he stood up he pocketed a page of pencilled figures he had compiled. Though normally they would have been reassuring, he was worried that he had missed something. The record of brandings had shown a steady increase each year so if the ranch was not losing calves, were they losing fully grown cattle? The books did not tally with the stories he had been hearing. The only explanation that came to him was that the rustlers, for some reason, had left the Diamond R alone.

Prudence came in with a cup of coffee and a slice of cake for him. He was trying hard to be friendly, but the maid still seemed ill at ease in his presence. 'Just what I needed, Prudence. I've had enough book work for today. After this I might go for a ride. Do you know the shortest way to Alder Creek?'

The maid looked even more worried than usual. 'Don't go over there, Mr Crossley. Those small ranchers might not give you a very good reception.'

'I doubt they'll trouble me much. I am not going with a team of armed men. I am hardly a threat to them. Do you know the closest ranch on Alder Creek?'

'That would be Coulters'. Mr Jensen don't like them folks much but others around here say they're honest enough.'

Though slightly annoyed by the fact that most westerners had trouble with his name, the company man forced himself to smile. 'There you go. You were worrying for nothing. Now which way to Alder Creek?'

The maid took him to the window and indicated a line of hills behind the ranch. 'Go through that notch you can see on the crest of the range and the first creek on the other side is Alder. When you hit it turn left and follow it down to Coulters'.'

Crossley-Hunt collected his horse and ignored the warnings of George, the old, crippled cowboy who did odd jobs around the ranch.

'You better be careful,' the old man said. 'Someone's shooting ranch folks. There's a killer out there and he could be after the first unlucky cuss to come along.'

The company man thanked him for his advice,

promised to be careful and cantered away. Two
hours later he turned his horse along Alder Creek.
He had enjoyed the ride and gradually he became
more relaxed. The Diamond R and its books
seemed to be a long way from where he was. He
had almost forgotten about rustlers when he
glimpsed horses moving through the trees ahead.
Sensing trouble, he undid the flap of his holster to
get quicker access to his Adams revolver. He had
carried the weapon through his military career
and saw no need to buy an American gun although
.450 ammunition for the Adams was sometimes
hard to find.

The riders came into view and he recognized
Connell but was surprised to see that his companion was very pretty girl. The deputy's pack horse
followed behind.

Crossley-Hunt halted his horse and waited for
them to come up to him. 'Hello, Connell,' he
greeted. 'Don't tell me you are eloping.'

'This is the one I was telling you about,' the
deputy said to his companion. 'This is Mr Crossley-
Hunt. He's from England on an inspection visit to
the Diamond R.' To the company man he said,
'This is Miss Mary Coulter. She's taking me to see
some of her neighbours. Her pa reckons there's
less chance of me getting my head blown off if she
is with me.'

Crossley-Hunt raised his hat. 'I'm very pleased

to meet you, Miss Coulter. I wonder if I might ride along with you because I also would like to meet some of your neighbours and I, too, don't want my head blown off.'

'It suits me,' Mary said.

Connell had been enjoying having the girl to himself and now felt slightly peeved that he would have to share her company, but could see the sense in Crossley-Hunt's proposal.

'That's an unusual name,' Mary observed. 'Does it have something to do with royalty?'

The company man laughed. 'Hardly. It appears that my grandfather married into the wealthy Crossley family and improved his chances of an inheritance by putting the Crossley in front of the plain old Hunt. The following generations have been saddled with this double-barrelled name ever since.'

'Out here we use first names mostly,' the deputy reminded him. 'What did your mother call you?'

'Clifford but Cliff will be fine. It sounds more rugged.'

The pun was lost on his companions, but they were Mary, Tom and Cliff as they rode together to the Sutton ranch. They failed to reach it.

The company man had just been advising the others the latest murder when they heard a horse whinny from behind some pines that screened a bend in the trail.

'Someone's coming,' Connell said.

Seconds later a party of horsemen came out of the trees, saw the trio and turned their mounts toward them. The foremost rider was a dark, buck-skin-clad individual on a roan pony. Directly behind him rode Sheriff McLeod and half-a-dozen men. The main posse had split with Raymond leading one group and Jensen and Coventry the other.

The sheriff did not look pleased to see Connell. 'So this is where you're hiding out,' the big lawman said accusingly. 'I reckoned you might have been out chasing rustlers but instead I find you socializing.' He glared at Mary. 'And with the enemy at that.'

'I don't consider Miss Coulter to be my enemy, Sheriff, and she has been helping me with my enquiries.'

'I'll bet,' leered a big cowhand sitting beside Adams. 'And what was fancy pants there helping you with?'

Crossley-Hunt saw the half smile on the Diamond R foreman's face telling him that trouble was not far away.

NINE

The company man could guess what had happened. Adams had set him up. The objectionable cowhand worked for another ranch so he had no power to fire him. It was a deliberate attempt to neutralize him and there was only one way that he could emerge with his reputation intact. Fully aware of what his reply would lead to, he addressed the big cowhand. 'You have a big mouth, my friend, but if it flaps open a bit more I might have to close it.'

McLeod added fuel to the fire. 'We're busy tracking a murderer, Mr Crawley-Hunt, otherwise I'd let you have a try at shutting Pecos's mouth. But for your sake and because there are more important things to do, we'll overlook your very indiscreet comments.' Secretly the sheriff knew that a confrontation was unavoidable, but he had to pretend that he was not one of the instigators.

60

'You are one very lucky Limey sonofabitch,' Pecos said. 'Next time we meet you won't have anyone to hide behind.'

Crossley-Hunt sounded almost tired. 'Right,' he told Pecos, as he stepped down from his horse. 'How do you want to settle this – guns or fists? '

'We can't have no shooting,' the sheriff objected. 'But if Mr Crawlin-Hunt is so set on getting his head ripped off his shoulders, I won't stop him. I doubt that we'll be delayed for long.'

The company man removed his coat, unbuckled his gunbelt and passed them to Connell. 'Hold these for a while, Tom.'

'Be careful, Cliff. There are no London prizing-ring rules here.'

'I should hope not,' Crossley-Hunt said calmly, as he turned to face his opponent.

Pecos handed his gun to Adams and with a smile on his face, advanced for what he expected to be a quick, easy victory. It was.

Crossley-Hunt lashed out as soon as he came into kicking range but his boot was aimed low. It took Pecos in the centre of the shin and the force straightened his foremost leg. As the leg straightened, his head involuntarily came down and forward to meet a rising right uppercut that smashed him upright again. It was a solid blow that staggered the big cowhand. But the Englishman gave him no time to recover. He jumped slightly in the air and with the full weight of his body behind it, drove the side of his foot into Pecos's left knee slamming the joint sideways and rupturing ligaments in the process. Pecos groaned aloud and staggered in an effort to meet the rush that was coming, but his knee would no longer support his weight. He was tottering on one foot when Crossley-Hunt feinted with his right and hooked a vicious left into his opponent's short ribs. The cowhand was halfway to the ground when a hard right took him on the jaw, snapped back his head and spun him as he fell. In seconds the fight was over.

An angry murmur broke out from the posse. 'You didn't fight fair,' a man accused.

'You're right – I didn't – and I don't. Any man who reckons he can hand me a whipping had better be able to do it. Would anyone else here like to try?'

'I wonder how good you are with a gun,' another man snarled.

'My friend,' Crossley-Hunt said mildly, 'Anyone who can't beat me with his fists certainly won't beat me with a gun. I was the best pistol shot of all the officers in my regiment.'

'But you ain't got a gun,' McLeod reminded, hoping that one of the onlookers would take the hint.

'I have,' Connell said. He was holding the

Adams revolver by the butt ready to shoot through the bottom of the holster if necessary. 'I don't mind trying out this English self-cocker if anyone gets a bit too ambitious.'

McLeod sought to regain control. 'There'll be no gunplay here. We have a murderer to catch.' He glared at Mary. 'You shouldn't be seeing things like this, young lady.'

'I agree, Sheriff,' she said with a pleasant smile. 'I didn't think you would let such a thing happen.'

At a loss for words, the sheriff turned to the men gathered around Pecos. 'How is he?'

'His knee's all swole up already,' Adams said. 'Could be something busted. He sure as hell won't be walking right for a while.'

'Get him on a horse and have a man take him home.' McLeod's eye fell on Connell. 'You can take his place. Your other duties are suspended till further notice.'

Connell said to Crossley-Hunt, 'Looks like there's been a change of plans. Will you escort Mary home?'

'I certainly will.'

The Englishman's enthusiastic reply caused a slight twinge of jealousy in the deputy. He told himself that such feelings were stupid as he had barely met the girl, but he had hoped for a chance to know her better.

The posse started off again. Chico rode a few

horse lengths ahead looking for tracks but found nothing. Occasionally he would halt and study something not apparent to the other posse members but then would ride on again. Connell soon reached the conclusion that the half-breed was putting on a show for the rest of the posse, probably making the job last to ensure better payment.

An hour later they met the two other groups at a prearranged spot. None had encountered anything suspicious. Jensen and Coventry had ridden across the smaller holdings along Alder Creek but learned nothing. The smaller ranchers had forted up on seeing them and admitted to nothing.

'They know,' Joe Raymond said angrily, 'but they won't tell us anything. They had guns on us from shuttered windows and would not show themselves. All we were told was to go away.'

Coventry gave a knowing smile. 'Be patient, Joe,' he said quietly, while casting a glance in Connell's direction, 'Don't do anything until you are sure that we have this new deputy where we want him.'

'I can tell you now where I want him,' Jensen muttered. 'I want him six feet under. He's thrown in with the enemy and he'll be nothing but trouble.'

'Wouldn't it be convenient if that skunk who's murdering our men should shoot Connell by mistake?' Coventry chuckled.

'Why stop at Connell?' Jensen suggested. 'Our company man from England is getting rather nosy too. We have work to do and he's holding things up. It would really strengthen our case against the rustlers if he should have an accident.'

Raymond looked worried. He removed his spectacles and polished them with his bandanna before saying, 'Don't get too impatient. Crossley-Hunt can't stay too long. He's a business manager. As long as the paperwork is right we can bamboozle him. If anything happens to him though there might be too many questions asked.'

Jensen said, 'Let's all head back to the Diamond R and stay the night. We can plan tomorrow's moves then.'

'What would McLeod's reaction be if his deputy met with a fatal accident?' Coventry asked.

Raymond muttered, 'He might not like it but would not look too hard for the killer if we told him not to. We own him body and soul and he knows it.'

The trio looked across to where the deputy was talking with some of the cowhands. The latter were being guarded in what they told him and none was particularly friendly, but it was a worry that men spoke to him at all because there was much to hide.

Connell felt that he had made some progress.

The cowhands would admit to nothing, but the odd careless word here and there indicated that the two men killed had been involved in the lynching of at least one of the alleged rustlers. He had a motive for the killings, but it pointed squarely at the small ranchers. Was this their way of hitting back against their more powerful enemies?

It was dark when the posse finally arrived back at the Diamond R and Jensen set about organizing food for the large number of unexpected guests. But he had one more task to perform. He told Adams, 'Find Chico. I have a job for him.'

'Are you sure you can trust him? That sneaky coyote would cut his own mother's throat for a nickel.'

'I'll be offering him a bit more than a nickel,' Jensen said.

TEN

Crossley-Hunt arrived half an hour after the posse. He had delayed at Coulter's ranch for longer than he had intended. Prudence had made sure that a meal was kept for him and he devoured it hungrily. It had been a long time since lunch.

The atmosphere inside the ranch house was decidedly frosty so the company man intended to seek out Connell who was sleeping outside with some of the other posse members. The night promised to be a cool one and he had returned to his room to collect his heavier coat when he noticed that a note had been pushed under the door. It was on a torn scrap of paper and written in crude block letters but the message was clear, CONEL IN DANGER.

Quickly folding the note he stuffed it in his pocket and hurried outside to find the deputy. He found him leaning on the top rail of a corral looking over the horses.

'How did things go with the Coulters?' Connell asked when the company man leaned on the rail beside him.

'I learned a lot, but I'm not here about that. I found this note pushed under my door tonight. It's too dark out here to read it but it says, CONEL IN DANGER. Whoever wrote it spelt your name wrong, but the message is clear enough.'

'Seems like I've trodden on some toes somewhere, or someone is worried that I know too much. I'm danged if I know what it is though. I'll need to watch my back while I'm in this nest of skunks and I reckon you might, too. What have you learned?'

Crossley-Hunt said quietly, 'Just by going on the books of the Diamond R, this whole rustling business has been exaggerated. Herd numbers seem to have been increasing at roughly the same rates each year. Either the rustlers are leaving this herd alone and concentrating on the others, or the whole story is wrong.'

'There is a very minor bit of rustling,' Connell said. 'That always happens in open-range country, but it is usually just someone killing for beef. Nobody these days is fool enough to drive off large numbers of branded stock and try to sell them. There might be a few calves wrongly branded, but that's only a spit in the ocean. A few mavericks might get branded illegally but it's a bit rich for the big ranchers to claim that all mavericks were descended from their herds. The Sioux wiped out the first ranch around here and their cattle ran wild so the mavericks are not all descendants of the stock that the big ranchers introduced later. My part in this is what is worrying me. I have been hired to handle a problem that doesn't really exist. The only reason I can see for me being here is that I might worry the small ranchers.'

'From what the Coulters told me, they're glad you are around. They were pleasantly surprised to find an impartial lawman.'

'It seems we have an unknown ally among the big ranchers,' Connell said. 'Do you have any idea at all who wrote that note?'

'Not a clue but take that warning seriously.'

'Thanks, I will – just one more thing. What do you know about those Black Angus cattle?'

Crossley-Hunt thought awhile. 'I know that since the first shipment in 1874 they are in great demand for American ranches. The Scots are getting big money for them. They are good for beef and they cross well with other breeds.'

'What do you know about cross-bred Angus cattle?'

'Very little. My job with the company is to over-see administration. I leave the technical details to the actual cattlemen. Will you be going out with the posse in the morning?'

'I expect so if I get through tonight without someone ventilating my hide. I'll camp a bit away from the ranch just to be on the safe side.'

Chico was a loner and did not mix much with the other members of the posse. He bedded down in the barn where no one would see him coming or going. Connell had slipped away quietly. He had been roaming around the yard of the ranch house one minute and was gone the next. Without wanting to draw too much attention to himself, the tracker checked the bunkhouse and, as far as he could, the main building, but there was no sign of the deputy. He knew that he would not be far away, but was also aware that Connell was on his guard. Jensen would not be happy, but Chico decided that searching for a wary man in the dark was just too risky a business. As the boss of the Diamond R had not paid him anything, he could hardly complain if the task was not completed immediately.

Jensen himself was having trouble sleeping. There were enough complications without the unexpected killing of the Double T men. Crossley-Hunt, though he probably did not know it, already had evidence that contradicted the claims about rustlers and Connell was sure to see the falsity of the claims. If there was one reason for optimism it was his expectation that the new deputy would soon be out of the game. Through the night Jensen wondered whether he would hear the shot that solved one of his problems.

When morning came, the ranch manager glanced out his window. The ranch horses were already corralled and cowhands and posse members were bustling about preparing for the new day. Jensen looked for Connell and did not see him at first. When he did he was both disappointed and alarmed. The deputy was walking around the fenced pasture behind the corrals where the new bulls were held. He tried to tell himself that Connell just had a cattleman's curiosity for a new breed but some inner voice told him that the deputy knew or suspected his secret. Dressing quickly, Jensen cursed Chico as he made his way to the main dining-room for breakfast.

The bulls were quiet and were used to human contact, consequently they took little notice as Connell moved among them. Without going too close he saw what he was seeking. He was walking toward the bunkhouse when the cook rang the triangle announcing to the cowhands that breakfast was ready. Connell had not been invited to dine at the ranch house with the sheriff and the other ranch bosses.

The cowhands complained, discussed horses or joked as each man collected a tin plate of bacon and beans and a mug of coffee from the cook. The kitchen was crowded and the others had no intention of making room for the deputy so he went out and sat on the porch. Another man also sat there: Chico.

'I saw you looking at them muley bulls,' the half-breed muttered as he chewed. 'What do you think of them?'

'They don't look anything special. I'm danged if I'd bring cattle like that all the way from Scotland.'

Chico chewed a bit more and said, 'Me neither. Real cattle have horns anyway. I wonder how those things will go in a bad winter.'

'They've proved they can stand up to rough conditions. The cold won't worry them.'

'It ain't only the cold,' Chico continued. 'There ain't gonna be much feed around when Coventry's cattle arrive.'

Connell stopped eating. 'Do you mean there are more cattle coming in here?'

'Sure are. There's fifteen hundred head comin' up from Texas. They'll be here in about a month. I know because I started out with them, but the trail boss is Coventry's son and he's as mean as his old man. I quit and came on ahead because I wanted to see some relatives of mine.'

'This country is overstocked now,' Connell said. 'A bad winter will wipe out a lot of cattle. How on earth does Coventry expect them to fit in?'

Chico swallowed the last of his breakfast and stood up. 'The way I figger it, he'll have to shift some of the cattle already here.' With that announcement he walked inside to dump his empty plate in the cook's wreck pan.

Connell finished his breakfast and went to saddle his horse. He found Sheriff McLeod engaged in the same task. 'Do you still want me with the posse today, Monty?' he asked.

'No. I think we are wasting our time. Chico can't seem to pick up any tracks and he's supposed to be good. What have you found out about them rustlers?'

'Do you know anyone around here who does rawhide work? I found a butchered steer with the hide missing.'

'You've only confirmed what someone else already knew. Jason Martel on Alder Creek used to make a lot of rawhide lariats, bosals, whips and hobbles and stuff like that. He used to make good money from it too, but the hides were not from the few head that he was running. He was the first rustler the vigilantes hanged.'

'And you have no idea where these vigilantes came from?'

'I haven't, and if the Good Lord gave you the sense of a gopher, you won't either. The rustlers are the problem, not the ones stopping them. You might as well go back to investigating those folks

73

along Alder Creek today. Just remember what side you're on. See me in Lodge Pole a week from now and you had better have a few results.'

'Don't worry,' Connell told him earnestly. 'I intend to get results.'

ELEVEN

The hunt for the murderer was scaled down. McLeod dropped the Diamond R men from the posse and departed. He would search back through the open range and the men from the Double T and Wineglass ranches would drop off as they reached their home bases.

Connell was about to depart when Crossley-Hunt walked across to where he was making the final adjustments on his pack. 'I see you got through the night in one piece, Tom,' he greeted. 'What are your plans now that the big murder hunt is over?'

'I'll ride around for a few days, but don't expect to find much. I report to Monty McLeod in about a week and then I reckon I'll be out of a job. When do you go back to England?'

'I'll have to think about it in a few days, but I'm in no hurry. I have spent so much of my life

75

outside the British Isles that I am not sure that I belong there anymore. I doubt that the non-existent rustler crisis will justify my remaining here much longer. Ollie Jensen will be happy to see the last of me.'

'There's one thing that might delay you a bit longer,' Connell suggested. 'It's those Angus bulls that the Diamond R paid so much for. I think that your company has been taken for a ride. The breed is new and not a lot is known about them in this country yet, but from the little I know, the Diamond R did not get what it paid for. Those are not good bulls and I think that they might not be pure-bred.'

The company man looked surprised. 'What makes you think that?'

'Some time ago I met an old Scot who came across with one of the early shipments. He told me that the breed is so strong that when crossed with other breeds the calves mostly look like the Angus. But if crossed with dairy breeds, they show a bit of orange inside the ears and inside the split of the hoofs. Those bulls have that orange and I think that they are cross-bred and not the pure-bred stock that your company paid for. They don't even look like good stock. A couple of those bulls have very poor conformation for a beef breed.'

'Are you sure? I know that a respected expert carefully selected the bulls in Scotland. If these are not the same bulls what happened the original ones?'

'That's a question you might need to ask. They might have been switched in Scotland, or they might have been switched after they landed here, but I would put my money on substitution somewhere along the way. My guess is that someone took, and probably sold, those very valuable bulls and switched them for cross-breeds. Whoever it was would know that the cattlemen here are unfamiliar with the breed and might not notice the difference.'

'Do you think Jensen could be involved in this?' the company man asked.

'I don't know. Be careful how you raise this because you are alone here with skunks like him and Adams. If they were involved and thought they were in danger of discovery, they'd kill you.'

'Tougher men than them have tried to kill me in several different countries, Tom. I'm not afraid of them.'

'Maybe,' Connell admitted, 'but then you had troops behind you and your enemies came from the front. I have to go now. Remember – be careful.'

From high on a heavily timbered ridge, Chico saw the deputy riding away from the Diamond R. The man and his horses seemed ant-like when viewed from that point, certainly too far for a rifle shot. I wonder what you're up to, he asked the distant horseman silently. What did Connell know that made Jensen want to kill him?

The half-breed returned to his pony. He would follow his man and see what he did. If the deputy met anyone, he would be interested in seeing who it was. Chico was playing a deadly game and liked to be sure of what was happening around him. Since McLeod had paid him off, there was no need for him to linger where he was but Chico had some killing to do.

Connell did not know that he was being watched but the very nature of his work made him cautious. He kept a watch on his back trail and changed direction regularly so that it would be hard for someone to determine where he was going and set an ambush.

Many cattle had died on the rangeland over the years and scavenging animals had often scattered their bones about. By examining all the carcasses he encountered, the deputy found another with a bullet hole in the skull. The hide was missing, another of Jason Martel's victims. The ears were still attached to the skull and both were intact. In the absence of earmarks, it was certain that the animal had been a maverick. It appeared that Martel had not been killing indiscriminately and in this case he had taken the hide from an ownerless cow.

Aware that the three big ranches were claiming all mavericks he thought that the number of such animals might have made rustling a paying proposition but he doubted it. The only unbranded stock he saw were small calves following branded mothers. These would be collected in the fall roundup.

Connell was giving his horses a drink at a creek when he saw two riders approaching. They were riding straight at him and did not appear to be in a hurry, but something about their approach warned the deputy that their intentions were not friendly. The deputy lifted his horse's head and turned toward the newcomers. 'Howdy,' he said.

His greeting was not returned.

The foremost rider, a hard-faced young man in a faded red shirt halted his horse a couple of yards away. Jesse Quinn was a bully at the best of times and with the odds in his favour, he was worse. With his right hand resting on his gun butt, he demanded, 'What are you doing here? This is Double T range.'

Connell could see trouble looming but ignored the question. 'This is open range,' he said evenly. 'The Double T range, what there is of it, is miles to the north. I have as much right here as you do. I don't think Joe Raymond would like to see his men rousting strangers. Does he know you are doing this?'

The mention of his boss might have caused a wiser man to reconsider, but Quinn, who considered himself an up-and-coming gunfighter, was eager for action. This stranger would be the first man he killed in a stand-up gun battle.

'We're asking the questions here,' the second man said. He was also young with straggly, shoulder-length fair hair. 'There's been a couple of our men murdered around here, and you might just be the *hombre* that's doing it. So you'd better start giving us answers, or you won't be riding away from here.'

'My name is Tom Connell. I'm a deputy hired by the Cattlemen's Association to investigate rustling.'

'And I'm President Grant,' the long-haired one mocked. 'Now hand over your gun or start shooting.'

Something about the pair warned Connell that both were in a murderous frame of mind, so, with little choice, he chose the latter option.

But he did not react as the others were expecting. He drove his heels into his horse jumping it forward to the right of the pair. This forced them to twist in their saddles and placed one cowboy in the other's line of fire.

All three grabbed for their guns. The deputy's sudden move took Quinn by surprise but the cowhand's Remington .44 had cleared the holster in a fraction of a second. By doing the unexpected, Connell got away the first shot. The bullet burned along the man's ribs. He flinched slightly sending his shot at the deputy wide of the mark. While he was trying to bring his horse under control, he fired again but everything was against accurate shooting and once more he missed. Long Hair started firing although his companion was partially between himself and his target.

The scene became a blur of plunging horses, gunsmoke and shots ringing out. Connell had no idea how many times he had fired until the hammer clicked on a fired shell. He had switched targets when he saw the red-shirted man reeling in the saddle. Through a cloud of powder smoke he saw that the long-haired man was on his face on the ground and the one in the red shirt was slowly sliding from his horse as the animal danced nervously about. He hit the ground and moved feebly, choking on the blood that was coming from his mouth.

The deputy wasted no time celebrating his survival. He holstered his gun and debated grabbing the Winchester from his saddle but saw that it would not be needed. Both men's fallen guns were in full view and neither was in a position to use them. He dismounted quickly and hurried across to the men on the ground.

Even as he reached Quinn, the man's eyes rolled back in his head, blood trickled from his mouth and he was beyond any help.

A glance told him that the other man was also dead. Though he had not been aiming at Long Hair's head, Connell saw that one of his bullets had struck him in the forehead. He had very nearly missed him.

The red-shirted one had a bloody furrow along his ribs, a broken left arm and a gaping bullet wound in his chest, Puzzled by the size of the hole the deputy turned the man over. To his surprise, he found a much smaller bullet hole. A slug had hit him just near the spine and torn through his body. The big hole in his chest was an exit wound. The man had been shot in the back and with something more powerful than a .45 Colt bullet.

He glanced about and saw a pine thicket about seventy yards away but there was no sign of movement. No black powder burns showed on the back of the red shirt as would have been the case if he had moved into his friend's line of fire. Connell suddenly had the chilling thought that a fourth person had intervened in the battle. If that was the case, which side had the mystery shooter taken? The three antagonists had been close together and moving about. Had the hidden shooter accidentally hit the wrong man?

Just in case the shooter was still there, he stepped behind his horse to reload his Colt before drawing his Winchester from the saddle boot. He was almost certain that the fourth man had fled the scene but advanced cautiously from one piece of cover to the next. There had been ample time for the hidden man to shoot him in the period immediately after the gun battle if he had wished to do so, but Connell was in no mood to take chances.

TWELVE

Connell quickly found where the rifleman had hidden. The shooter had hitched his horse to a nearby tree and fired through a screen of berry bushes. A brass shell caught his eye. He picked it up and saw that it had been from a .45/.75 Centennial model Winchester, a weapon much more powerful than the .44/.40 favoured by most ranch men. The ground showed enough prints for him to see that the rifleman had not been lying in wait to ambush someone at the creek. He had arrived at the scene, observed what was happening, taken a shot and fled as soon as he saw that he had hit someone.

Returning to the horses, he was attempting to hoist one of the dead men across the saddle of a very nervous horse when he heard riders behind him. Expecting to see more Double T men, he drew his carbine and stood behind his horse. As

the riders came nearer he recognized two of the
ranchers who had brought Murphy's body into
Lodgepole. The newcomers also recognized him
and slowed their mounts to a walk.

'What in the hell happened here?' asked Bill
Sutton.

His companion, George Norton looked at the
deputy suspiciously but said nothing.

'Two men from the Double T jumped me at the
creek,' Connell explained. 'I shot one, but someone with a rifle over there in the trees, put a bullet
through the one in the red shirt. Do you know
them?'

Sutton looked at the closest dead man. 'His
name's Jesse Quinn. He's no loss – liked to think
he was a gunman.'

'The other one's name is Willing, or something
like that,' Norton volunteered. 'I've seen him at
round-ups. He's no loss either.'

'Seems like you and someone else did this
district a big favour, Connell,' Sutton said.

'There's one thing I need to clear up, gents.
What sort of rifles are you carrying?'

Slightly puzzled they produced the long arms
they each had on their saddles. Sutton had a
Henry .44 rim fire in a rawhide loop on his saddle
horn and Norton had a Winchester .44/.40.
Connell explained about the shell he had picked
up and asked if they knew anyone who had an

1876 Model Winchester. Both shook their heads.

'Those Winchester Express calibres are a bit out of the price range of us small ranchers,' Norton told him. 'Now, what are you going to do with these dead *hombres?*'

'If you'll give me a hand to get them on their horses. I'll take them to the Double T.'

Sutton was aghast. 'If you go to the Double T with two of Raymond's dead cowhands, you might not come out again. That four-eyed sonofabitch is likely to shoot you when he sees that Quinn was shot in the back. Take the bodies to town and let McLeod break the news to Raymond.'

'It's a long ride,' Connell argued.

Norton agreed. 'It is, but at least you'll live to get there. You might think you're the law around here, but Raymond and the other pair run the whole show. McLeod takes their word for everything. If one of them was to shoot you – and that's on the cards – he'd just cook up a story and the sheriff would go along with him.'

Sutton added, 'There have been two small ranchers lynched around here and we believe that men from all three ranches were involved. There could be more than a dozen murderers on those three spreads and if they thought you were getting too close, your life would not be worth a plugged nickel.'

'Thanks for the warning,' Connell told them. 'If

you'll give me a hand in getting this pair across their saddles, I'll take my chances with McLeod. Tell your neighbours what happened here too. There are bound to be some wild stories flying about.'

Crossley-Hunt knew that Jensen was hiding something when he started discussing the imported bulls. The ranch manager was going to great lengths to avoid discussing the deal in any detail. He seemed to recall little about the transaction and maintained that most of it had been arranged between the English company and a livestock agent based in Chicago. He suggested that the company man should call in at Loeb Livestock in Chicago on his way home if he wanted to be fully briefed on the importation details.

Though he already knew the livestock agent's address, Crossley-Hunt made a careful note of it for Jensen's benefit. The latter pretended that he was not worried, but inwardly he was fighting down panic. He cursed Connell silently for he was sure that he had sown the seeds of suspicion in the company man's mind. The knowledge that Chico had missed killing Connell also did little to improve his humour. He left the office and walked out to the kitchen. 'Prudence,' he bellowed.

The little woman appeared nervously at the door with a broom still in her hands.

'Get Ed Adams to see me. Don't stand there like a lost sheep. Get moving.'

The woman looked panic-stricken, turned and hurried away.

Ten minutes later the foreman strolled in. 'You wanted to see me about something, Ollie?'

'Where's Chico?'

'Hell, I don't know. It was McLeod hired him, not us. He could be in Lodgepole getting drunk by now.'

'Send a couple of the boys out and find the ugly little coyote. Tell him I have an urgent job for him.'

Adams looked at his boss shredly. 'The boys might not find Chico. He comes and goes as it suits him. But do you really need him? Some of us reckon he led the posse around in circles when we were looking for Schultz's killer. I wouldn't trust that sneaky varmint as far as I could throw him. What can he do that I can't? I don't mind earning a bit of extra money on the side.'

'Would you kill a man for two hundred dollars?'

Adams gave a slight chuckle. 'Hell, Ollie, if it's the one I'm thinking of, I'd kill him for practice but two hundred bucks would be nice.'

Suddenly Jensen felt better. He had Chico stalking Connell and Adams would be after Crossley-Hunt. His secret would be safe and the rustlers of Alder Creek would be blamed.

Unaware of the plot against him, the company man saddled a horse. He wanted to get away from the unfriendly atmosphere at the ranch and the friendliest face he could imagine was that of Mary Coulter.

The foreman let Crossley-Hunt ride away and hurried to his horse as soon as his intended victim was out of sight. He would be easy to track and the country into which he was headed afforded ample spots for an ambush.

The company man steered straight across a mile of open, grassy flats and set his mount up the steep ridge to the west. The higher ground was rocky and barren and partially covered in stunted pines and cedars. There was no feed or water there and the cattle rarely ventured over it. The ridge formed a natural barrier between the Diamond R and the ranches along Alder Creek. As his mount climbed higher, the rider could see miles of open grassland below him, dotted with the tiny forms of grazing cattle. He remembered then what Connell had told him about the country being overstocked. Though the stock he had passed were in good condition, he knew that things would be different when snow covered the bit of dry, brown grass that still survived. He did not need much experience with cattle to know that the Diamond R had a big part in the overcrowding of the open range.

Once over the ridge, he began the descent into

the valley of Alder Creek. More timber grew on that side and he could not see any buildings, but a column of smoke rising above the dark green of the pines indicated the location of the Coulter ranch. He tried to convince himself that his visit was strictly business but found himself hoping that Mary would be home.

Adams had been trailing at a distance but once his intended victim was on the other side of the hill, he urged his horse into a gallop to bring him into closer range. When he saw the chimney smoke, the foreman guessed where Crossley-Hunt was going and turned his mount along the top of the ridge. He knew the country well and now intended a short cut that would take him ahead of the Englishman. For half a mile he followed the ridge line and then turned down the slope. He took things more slowly then and the fallen pine needles muffled the sound of his horse. Eventually though, he found the spot he was seeking.

A spur ran off the main ridge descending where Alder Creek looped toward it. A rider following the worn path beside the stream would pass within a hundred yards of the spur's lower slopes. He could conceal his horse behind a screen of pines and bushes and would have open ground between his position and the creek's edge.

There was no hint of a wind and the horses were unlikely to scent each other and betray the ambush with a whinny of greeting. Carefully Adams eased a cartridge into his rifle's breech, checked his sight settings and settled down to wait. He knew that the wait would not be a long one.

It seemed no time at all before he glimpsed movement among the trees and a short time later, Crossley-Hunt rode into his sights.

THIRTEEN

Connell's entry into town with two dead men in tow certainly gave its citizens a new subject for conversation. Some just stared as he passed but others followed him along the sides of the street hoping to learn more about the strange sight.

Roberts saw him coming and hurried outside. 'Connell,' he said almost as though he did not believe his own eyes. 'What in the hell are you doing?'

'I'm delivering a couple of dead men to town. Where's McLeod?'

'He ain't here. I think he's out at the Wineglass with Coventry. What happened? Who are they?'

'I'll tell you when we get inside. Now, where do I put the late lamented until McLeod can see them?'

'Bring them round the back. There's a shed we can lock them in. I know they ain't likely to get out,

92

but I don't want curious folks getting in.'

'I know them fellers,' one of the onlookers said. 'That's Quinn and Willing. They work for the Double T. The brand's there on the horses.'

'Well they don't work there now,' another told him. 'Looks like they had some rustler trouble.'

The two deputies worked quickly, first securing the bodies and then unsaddling the horses before turning them loose in the sheriff's corral.

Pushing away curious onlookers, Roberts ushered Connell through the back door of the building and following him inside, locked it. Then, turning to the new deputy, he demanded, 'Tell me what happened.'

Connell explained the situation and a look of disbelief came over his colleague's beefy face. He thought it too much of a coincidence that two different men, unknown to each other, could be shooting at the dead men at the same time. He plainly disbelieved Connell's guess that the bullet that killed Quinn was intended for himself and the dead man might accidentally have moved into the line of fire.

Minutes later McLeod came bustling through the door. 'What's this about a shooting?' he demanded, as he placed his black hat on a wall rack.

Again Connell repeated the story and again his account was greeted with disbelief. He eyed the new deputy suspiciously. 'Are you sure you didn't shoot Quinn in the back while he was running away?'

'Damn sure. He was hit by a .45/.75 and I have the shell to prove it. My .44/.40 would not have made an exit hole the size of the one in Quinn even if it had gone right through. Those express rifles are for big game and long-range shooting.'

Roberts asked, 'Should I get one of the locals to ride out to the Double T and tell Joe Raymond?'

'Yes,' McLeod replied. 'Tell anyone who wants to go that it is worth a dollar. But don't give the messenger too many details. There's a lot about this that we don't know yet.'

Crossley-Hunt was steering his horse around a pine sapling and the slight change of direction was enough to throw off the rifleman's aim. The bullet that should have knocked the company man from the saddle clipped a lock of mane from his horse's neck. The startled animal gave a sideways jump and the rider's leg became entangled in the sapling. A branch swung into Crossley-Hunt's face and he was dragged from the saddle as the frightened horse bounded away. He hit the ground hard and was temporarily winded but instinctively he took the precautions that his army experience had taught him. He rolled sideways down the creek bank.

Adams was not sure that he had scored a hit as he did not hear the distinctive sound of the bullet striking that a body hit usually produced. He saw Crossley-Hunt roll over the edge of the creek bank, but thought that the force of his fall might have given him the necessary impetus. The rifleman worked the loading lever of his carbine and sighted on the creek bank. If his target showed, he would be waiting.

Gasping for breath, the company man slid down the creek bank, but was able to stop himself before slipping into the water. He drew his revolver from its holster then crawled along below the level of the bank not daring to peer over it until he found cover behind a small bush that grew on the upper edge. He took a couple of deep breaths, removed his hat and cautiously raised his head behind the leafy screen. His view of the hillside was obstructed by the foliage before him and he saw no sign of his attacker. Fifty yards away his horse had stopped after treading on the fallen reins but he would have to cross too much open ground to get to it. He decided to wait until he saw the rifleman's next move.

Adams thought he had hit the Englishman but was not sure. He decided to wait a little longer, leaving the riderless horse where it was for bait. If the company man was uninjured or slightly wounded, the foreman thought that his quarry would try to reach his mount to make his escape. If nothing happened in the next few minutes, he would approach and check on the result of his shot.

In his years on India's North-west Frontier, Crossley-Hunt had been shot at many times by hostile tribesmen and was more experienced in such situations than his attacker. The mixture of impatience and curiosity had been the downfall of many a Pathan sniper so he lay still, watching and waiting. The range was too long for his revolver and it was safer to let the shooter come to him rather than vice versa. He knew that a man moving was the one at a disadvantage, so he waited.

Adams, in the minutes that passed, convinced himself that he was being unnecessarily cautious and stole from his position. But he moved carefully and stayed under cover as much as possible. Halfway to the creek bank a loose rock rolled out from under his foot and bounced down the slope. It betrayed his presence but brought no hostile response.

The sound alerted Crossley-Hunt and he was concerned to see that the man with the rifle was approaching from an unexpected angle and would see him in a few more steps. Firing double-action, he triggered three quick shots. At least one took effect and the Diamond R foreman was twisted a little to the side as the bullet struck him. But he remained on his feet and, firing his carbine from the hip, replied with a shot that kicked dirt in his opponent's face. Then he felt the effect of the wound to the thigh and retired behind a convenient stump.

Crossley-Hunt also rolled sideways to the better cover of a slight bend in the creek bank. Quickly he flipped open his revolver's loading gate and one by one, punched out the empty shells, replacing each with a fresh cartridge from his ammunition pouch.

Adams had a fleeting glimpse of a target and fired a hasty shot that came too close for comfort. Crossley-Hunt fired back quickly, one shot going wide and the other thudding into the stump that protected his opponent. The foreman took another chance, exposing himself momentarily and ducking behind cover when the company man shot at him. He had been counting the Englishman's shots. 'You're empty,' he shouted triumphantly, and began a limping run at his man, firing the carbine from the hip as he approached.

Crossley-Hunt ignored the inaccurate shot and took careful aim as Adams advanced, working the loading lever for a killing shot. Firing single-action, he placed his first shot in the centre of the foreman's chest. His face a mask of shock, Adams seemed not to believe what was happening. He was trying to fire his rifle again when another bullet struck him in almost the same place and he pitched forward on his face.

Cautiously, the company man advanced keeping his gun trained on the fallen man. With his foot, he carefully moved the Winchester out of his adversary's reach although he knew that it was probably an unnecessary precaution. Even before turning the body over, the company man knew who it was: the Diamond R would need a new foreman.

He was reloading his revolver when he heard horsemen approaching. Uncertain as to the identity of the newcomers, he grabbed the dead man's carbine and stepped back to better cover below the creek bank. Two riders rode out of the trees, Ben Coulter and his son, Bob.

Ben looked at the Englishman and the dead man nearby. 'We heard shooting. What's going on here?'

Crossley-Hunt indicated his English revolver. 'You could say it was a family disagreement. One Adams just met another. Our trusted foreman just tried to kill me. I knew he didn't like me but didn't expect that he would resort to murder.'

'He was always a mean cuss,' Coulter said. 'He's no loss except to Ollie Jensen. He'll have to do his own dirty work now.'

'Are you implying that Jensen could be behind this attempt?'

The rancher leaned his hands on the saddle horn. 'Ed Adams didn't have too many original ideas of his own. Ollie Jensen usually pulled his strings. Have you been upsetting Jensen about something?'

Crossley-Hunt looked puzzled. 'I can't recall any disagreement that warranted a murder, but I doubt that he'll be pleased by the result of this afternoon's work.'

'Joe Raymond on the Double T will be a lot less pleased,' Coulter told him. 'Not real far from here yesterday, Tom Connell had a run-in with two of Raymond's men. Tom shot one and some unknown but public-spirited citizen, let daylight into another. There's been a regular epidemic of lead poisoning around here in the last few days but I'm glad to see that the other side are now taking the casualties.'

'I'd better get going, Coulter. I have to take Adams's body back to the ranch.'

The rancher shook his head. 'Don't do that. Take him to Sheriff McLeod in town. You need a few witnesses around you, because you're not dealing with the most upright of citizens. Come home with me and have a square meal. Then we'll deliver old Ed here to the sheriff. It will be an all night ride but I'll guide you there. I'll send young Bob to the Diamond R with a note from you so that Jensen will be in the picture.'

Mickey Lonsdale and Noah Hutchins were worried men. They had just heard of the deaths of the two cowhands who had not returned to the Double T the previous night. Quinn's death disturbed them the most.

Lonsdale's face suddenly looked older than its twenty-two years and a frightened look in his darting eyes showed that he was close to panic. 'I'm seein' Raymond tonight and snatching my time,' he said. 'They're catchin' up with us. You and me, Noah, we're the only ones left. If we stay around here we'll end up like Cutler and Schultz and Quinn.'

Hutchins, slightly older and taller was as uneasy as his companion, but was not so sure what he would do. 'Raymond ain't going to like us leaving. He'll only have the cook and Hoppy Ferris left – no working cowhands.'

'That's his problem. He was happy to have us go off hangin' anyone we suspected of bein' rustlers, but he's doin' nothing to protect us now. We were promised the full protection of the law but that did nothing at all for the others.'

As he spoke, Lonsdale walked to the bunkhouse door and looked out at the sun as it hovered on the top of a distant mountain range and threw its last long shadows across the land. A rifle crashed and he might have seen the red muzzle flash that stabbed from the deep shade on a nearby hill but only the stricken man would ever know. A big express bullet with the tip scored to make it break up had torn into his lower abdomen and punched his doubled-over body back through the open doorway.

Hutchins stared for a second, jumped over the fallen man and attempted to slam shut the door. A second shot went through the pine as though it was cardboard. Splinters flew from the back of the door as the 350 grain slug started to deform before continuing its path through the cowhand's body scattering broken pieces of bullet as it went.

Chico hurried back to where he had left his horse. He was not sure of his second hit but would be able to find out soon enough.

FOURTEEN

Monty McLeod looked skywards as if seeking an angel to come down and solve his problems. But as his jurisdiction did not extend upwards, he was forced to contend with the dilemma himself. 'These ranch crews are being decimated,' he bellowed at Crossley-Hunt. 'You're shooting cowhands, Connell's shooting cowhands. There's a crazy sonofabitch out there shooting cowhands and even young Coulter has tried his hand at shooting cowhands. Why isn't someone shooting rustlers for a change?'

'Could it be that ranch employees are easier to find than rustlers?' the Englishman asked. He seemed to be enjoying the sheriff's frustration.

'I've got a good mind to arrest you for murder, Crossley, or whatever you call yourself'

'If you had arrested the men who lynched those alleged rustlers, Sheriff, this problem might not have occurred. I notice none of them reported the killing to you. Adams tried to kill me and I defended myself. I will continue to defend myself through your legal system with all the resources of my employer if such action becomes necessary.'

Any further discussion was cut short when Connell walked into the office. He was surprised to see the company man in town, but was even more surprised when he heard the reason for his visit. 'I knew that you and Adams didn't get along,' he said, 'but I didn't expect him to be taking shots at you.'

Crossley-Hunt had his own ideas but was reluctant to express them in the sheriff's presence. 'You never can tell with some people,' he said cautiously. 'But right now if Sheriff McLeod has no more objections, I have two horses to care for and will have to get a room for the night. I'll return to the Diamond R tomorrow.'

'Wait a while and I'll come with you. What I have to do won't take long.' Connell dipped into his pocket as he spoke and tossed a cheap metal star on the sheriff's desk. 'Here's my badge, Sheriff. I'm quitting.'

Though taken by surprise. McLeod was not greatly upset. The new deputy had posed unexpected problems. Nevertheless he demanded, 'Why?'

'I don't like taking money under false pretences.

103

I was hired to solve a rustling problem and there is none. Someone is playing games and I want no part of it. Either the Cattlemen's Association are being played for fools or they are in some sort of dirty deal. People are prepared to kill just to conceal what is really happening here. I don't intend to be a hired gun for those who are behind all this murder.'

Anger flashed across the sheriff's face. 'Are you implying that I'm working for murderers? What are you being paid to throw in with the rustlers?'

'I'm glad you mentioned pay, McLeod, because I have some money coming, two weeks' pay plus the allowance for using my own horses. How do I go about getting it?'

'If it was left to me, Connell, you'd get nothing, but I'll get you a cheque in the morning. It has to be counter-signed by a member of the Association. Jack Coventry's coming to town tomorrow and I'll get him to do it. Now if that's all you need, you can get out of my office.'

'I'll come with you, Tom,' Crossley-Hunt said.

McLeod bellowed, 'I didn't say you could go anywhere.'

The Englishman looked him straight in the eye. 'Feel free to try stopping me any time you like. But I really would not advise it.' Then he turned about and walked out the door.

Connell watched until the company man had

left the office and backed out after him. He had seen the sheriff's hand almost involuntarily moving toward the butt of his gun and was not sure how well the big man could control his anger. He had a feeling that, given the opportunity, McLeod was quite capable of shooting a man in the back and concocting some sort of cover story afterwards.

The sheriff glared after the pair but dared not try to stop them. He had been around long enough to recognize dangerous men when he saw them. Then his gaze fell on Roberts watching wide-eyed from the corner of the room. 'Find Chico for me,' he ordered.

The big deputy shrugged his shoulders. 'Hell, Monty. He could be anywhere. He just comes and goes. I haven't seen him around for a couple of days.'

'Start asking around. Someone will know where he is.'

Connell took the Englishman to the local livery stable and waited while he arranged accommodation for the two Diamond R horses. When Crossley-Hunt had attended to that task, he suggested that he spend the night at the shack he had been allowed to use while in town. It had a spare bunk and they would be able to discuss matters away from any eavesdroppers.

The company man agreed and, as the town's

only restaurant was closed, he was happy to accept the invitation to a meal as he had not eaten for many hours.

They had almost reached the shack when a horseman came down the road. Connell recognized the wiry, ambling pony that Chico had ridden when he was with the posse. Though plain in appearance, the little roan had a long-striding walk that left many bigger horses behind. It was too dark to recognize the rider and if he saw them he gave no sign of recognition, but both men knew it was Chico.

'I wonder what he's been up to,' Crossley-Hunt said quietly. 'I don't altogether trust that man.'

'You and me both,' Connell agreed. 'While we were at the Diamond R, he let slip to me that Coventry has fifteen hundred cattle on the trail and heading this way. He might have been stringing me along, or might have just been careless, but close-mouthed characters like that usually don't say things they don't want other folks to know.'

Later that night as they were about to turn in, they heard a horse come pounding up the street.

'There's trouble,' Connell said. 'Nobody gallops like that in the dark without a good reason.'

Next morning they found out the reason. The messenger was a cowboy from the Diamond R. Their foreman Ed Adams and Crossley-Hunt the English supervisor had not returned to the ranch.

A frantic messenger from the Double T had also advised Jensen that two men had died in an attack on the ranch leaving the Double T with no working cowhands. The boss of the Diamond R was seeking to raise a posse to rid the area once and for all of rustlers.

Coventry was strutting around the sheriff's office like a bantam rooster when Crossley-Hunt and Connell went there in the morning. He glared at the latter as he came in. 'The sheriff tells me you've sold out, Connell. You had a big reputation but it will be a pretty poor one after I'm finished with it.'

The former deputy tried a shot in the dark. 'My reputation will be better than yours when the other ranchers find out about those extra cattle coming in on a range that is already overstocked.'

The little rancher was visibly shocked and the surprised reaction from McLeod showed that he, too, was disconcerted by the news. His thin lips compressed for a moment as if to stifle an unguarded comment. When Coventry finally spoke, he said lamely, 'I don't know what you're talking about.'

'That's good,' Connell said cheerfully. 'It's nice to know that you are not a range-grabbing skunk. Now if you'll countersign that cheque that the sheriff is holding, I'll be on my way.'

McLeod glared at Crossley-Hunt. 'What are you doing here?'

'I still have a responsibility to the Diamond R. After arranging a funeral for Adams, I intend to collect the cowhand who brought the message and our late foreman's horse and return to let Jensen know what's going on.'

'Will you be joining the posse?'

'That depends upon the posse's intentions. If we are after those who attacked the Double T, I will. But if this posse is intended simply to wage war on the smaller ranches, I won't be with you, nor will any man in my company's employment.'

'But we need those men. Raymond has no hands left and I can only spare a few. You don't know how things are here,' Coventry protested.

Crossley-Hunt replied, 'I don't think anyone really knows that. But one thing is sure, the situation is more complex than just a matter of rustling. Now if you will excuse me. I'll be getting about my business.'

Outside the office, the company man asked Connell, 'Will you be moving on now?'

'Eventually, but first I'm going to warn the small ranchers to expect trouble. If they'll trust me, I might hang around a while until all this blows over. Watch your back, Cliff, because I don't think Adams came after you on his own account.'

'I agree with you there; you and I could both be marked men. Remember that note that was slipped under my door? Where can I find you if I need you?'

Connell thought a while. 'We might be able to keep contact through the Coulters.'

A knowing smile came to Crossley-Hunt's face. 'Of course, the presence of Mary Coulter would not have anything to do with that idea.'

'I hardly know the girl,' Connell said defensively, as he mounted his horse. 'Watch your back.'

FIFTEEN

Mary Coulter steered her pony along a narrow ridge that offered a good view of the grasslands on both sides. It was against her parents' better judgement that she was out alone when such tension existed in the community. A range war was brewing, the pessimists said, for news of the attack on the Double T had spread and the larger ranchers were sure to hit back. Her brother Bob was several miles away on the southern end of the same range of hills.

Their father was gathering a force of small ranchers together ready to meet any threat that their youthful lookouts sighted.

Mary spotted Connell when he and his two horses were a single dot in the distance. It was some time before she could discern any details and at first she wondered if she should report the newcomer's presence. Then she recognized the

110

horse that the former deputy was riding. Its white blaze and bright chestnut coat showed distinctly in the clear morning air. Much relieved, she rode down off the ridge on a course that would intercept the former deputy. In doing so, she failed to notice another tiny dot in the distance.

Chico would have stayed on Connell's trail if the sun had not caught a silver concho on the bridle of Mary's pony. Someone was on the crest of the range ahead. With the instincts of a man who had been hunted before, he changed course riding into the pines around the base of the hills. He already had a fair idea where Connell was going and it was safer to avoid observation than to stay on his tracks. He would climb the range on its rougher, northern end where the person on the crest could not see him.

Connell saw the grey pony and its rider coming toward him through the timber on the slope. Resisting the urge to hurry, he held his horse at the same rapid walk until they met.

'Howdy, Tom,' the girl greeted cheerfully. 'Are you back after rustlers again?'

'Not this time, Mary. I'm out of a job. I quit yesterday. I figured though that Ben and the others should know that trouble is headed this way. Coventry and McLeod are raising a posse. Two of Joe Raymond's cowhands have been murdered and it's not hard to guess who is being blamed.'

'Is the Diamond R supplying men for the posse?'

'Cliff is agreeable as long as they don't ride in here shooting. I think he's trying to keep control even though the hands are loyal to Jensen.'

Mary frowned. 'Why would it benefit small ranchers like us to kill men on the Double T? They're no worse than the others and the Diamond R is much closer. It's more likely that someone has a grudge against Joe Raymond and his men.'

'Were they in any way connected to the lynchings that were going on here?'

'There have been rumours to that effect, but nobody knows for sure.'

'If they are right,' Connell said seriously, 'someone on your side has a good motive for murder. That same person might also just like killing people so it might not be a good idea for you to be out here alone.'

'I'm out here watching for that posse you came to warn us about. Pa was one jump ahead of you. He reckoned that the Association would hit back at us after they lost so many men recently. My brother Bob's at the other end of this range just in case they come from that direction. They won't catch us by surprise when they come.'

'I don't like you being out here alone with a killer loose, Mary.'

A determined look came across the girl's face. 'Maybe you don't, Tom, but I have a job to do. I'll be careful. If you are looking for Pa, you'll find him and the others at the big flat along the creek. Just go over the range and turn south when you hit the creek.'

'I'll do that,' Connell said. 'Meanwhile, you be careful.'

Barely a quarter-mile away, Chico sat quietly among the trees watching as Connell rode away. At first he thought that the girl had been waiting for the former deputy until it dawned on him that she was watching for McLeod's posse. He had deliberately made himself scarce to avoid recruitment. He would need more freedom of movement to kill his next man.

Crossley-Hunt, with two cowhands, arrived at the Double T before the riders coming from town and the Wineglass ranch. He found Raymond scarcely daring to move outside the house. The attack on the ranch had shattered his confidence. His workforce had been reduced to a cook and a semi-crippled odd job man. His foreman and four cowhands were all dead and left him with the distinct impression that he was also on the killer's list. It would be impossible to guard against a long-range rifle shot and Raymond knew it.

'Come into the house,' the rancher said

nervously when the others had ridden up. 'There's a madman loose and you could be a target outside.'

The Englishman followed Raymond inside and was amazed at how much the man had deteriorated since their last meeting. The aggressive self-confidence was gone and fear was now ruling his life. Though not expecting to hear the truth, he asked the rancher, 'Why do you think that your men have been singled out by this killer?'

'It's because it was my turn.'

'Your turn – for what – to get killed?'

'I forgot – you wouldn't know. It doesn't matter.' Raymond was suddenly aware that in his distress, he had said too much. The sound of horses outside saved him further embarrassment. 'Sounds like the others are here,' he said hastily.

Dust swirled around the ranch-house yard as McLeod, Roberts, Coventry and half-a-dozen men brought their horses to a halt.

The sheriff dismounted as Raymond and Crossley-Hunt emerged from the house. He greeted Raymond but ignored the Englishman. 'Now, Joe,' he continued. 'Show me where all this shooting took place.'

'You might need someone good at trailing,' Raymond told him. 'Is Chico with you?'

McLeod shook his head. 'No. The shiftless little sonofabitch has wandered off somewhere. Like all 'breeds, he's never there when he's needed. I can track a bit if I have to. Now let's see where everything happened.'

The sheriff examined where the two cowhands had been standing and expressed some surprise at the hole in the bunkhouse door. By sighting through the hole he was able to determine the approximate location of the shooter. Leaving the others, he walked up into the trees and soon found where the rifleman had been. Two long brass shells from a .45/.75 showed that he had the right place. Calling for the others to bring the horses, McLeod followed a trail of hoofprints and overturned stones up the ridge to its crest. He was panting heavily when he reached the summit and had been forced to stop several times to catch his breath. The ground was stony in places and it was only by close examination that he could see where the horse had been.

A black tail hair caught in a bush was no help in determining the colour of the killer's horse as many different coloured horses had black manes and tails. The hoofprints also told him little. They were around average size but the animal could have been a pony with larger than usual feet or a big horse with small feet as many quarter horses were.

'We're hardly likely to catch up with the killer at the rate we're going,' Coventry complained. 'Let's think ahead. We can cross over to Alder Creek and see if we pick up those tracks again. I'm sure that's where our killer came from.'

McLeod was not so convinced. 'I don't know, Jack. Those tracks are so blamed ordinary that I might not recognize them again. There's nothing distinctive at all about them.'

Raymond supported Coventry. Surrounded by armed men, his confidence had returned slightly. 'Jack's right. That killer came from the Alder Creek bunch. Let's turn the place inside out until we find a man with a .45/.75 Winchester. There are not a lot of those new rifles about.'

Crossley-Hunt spoke up then. 'Before you do that, give me a chance to talk to Coulter and the others. If I can talk them into cooperating it will save possible bloodshed.'

'If they know we are coming they're likely to ambush us,' Coventry protested. 'I'm not in favour of that at all.'

'Me neither,' Raymond announced. His confidence was growing by the minute.

'There's sure to be shooting if we just barge into those ranches,' the Englishman argued. 'I'm almost certain I can talk sense into these people. There's no need for anyone to get killed.'

'Frightened of a bit of blood?' Coventry taunted.

Crossley-Hunt turned on him and his face darkened with anger. 'No, I'm not frightened of a bit of blood. I've seen more blood and been shot at more times than the rest of you put together but in the process I have learned to value human life and will avoid killing where I can. In my army days I sometimes had to take orders from jackasses but those days are over. Now I'll do things my way.'

'I'm running this posse,' McLeod growled. 'I'm the law around here.'

'That may be, but I am taking myself and my two company employees out of your little army, Sheriff.' The company man called to the pair of Diamond R riders he had brought with him. 'I'm ordering you men to return to the ranch. If you don't you will both be out of a job when I get back.'

'If you get back,' sneered Deputy Roberts.

The two cowhands concerned looked uncertainly from McLeod to Crossley-Hunt.

'You two can't leave,' the sheriff announced. 'You're special deputies.'

'They weren't sworn in,' Crossley-Hunt told him. 'In fact, with the exception of your deputy, none of us has been sworn in. You men,' he told the pair of Diamond R hands, 'report back to Mr Jensen. Our ranch will not be involved in such a questionable operation. And now, Sheriff, I am going ahead to talk to the other ranchers. You can give me half an hour and follow, or you can shoot me in the back.'

Wheeling his horse, the Englishman cantered away. Apologetically the Diamond R men also turned for home.

Raymond's insecurity returned. 'Hell, Monty, we just lost three guns and the other side maybe gained one.'

'I can soon fix that,' Coventry said, as he drew his rifle from its saddle scabbard.

In a tired voice, McLeod said, 'Put it away, Jack. Those two Diamond R men are still close enough to see what happens. You'll have to kill them too. Let's hope them rustlers don't like that Limey sonofabitch as much as he thinks. One of them might shoot first and save us a big problem.'

'Are you going to give him a half-hour start?' Raymond asked impatiently.

'I was coming to that,' the sheriff said. 'We don't follow Crosscut. If we go up the north end of the range, he won't see us behind him and will think we have waited. We can set up a very nice ambush at the place where they come up from Alder Creek. There's cover for us, but anyone coming up that trail will be in the open as they go over the top. If those ranchers are riding out against us, we can slaughter them there.'

SIXTEEN

Mary had returned to her place on the crest of the range. She was bored and tired of staring into the distance. Had she been aware that Chico was still watching her from the trees she would not have been so relaxed.

The killer could not afford to reveal his presence and was also loath to move from the area as he was sure that it offered the best opportunity of intercepting his final victim. There was still a good chance that the girl would move away before the others arrived, so, with the patience of a born hunter, he settled down to wait.

A few minutes later, Mary saw Crossley-Hunt approaching although she was unsure at first as to his identity. She remained alert, ready to ride back to Alder Creek but then recognized the Englishman and relaxed. Though she did not know it, Connell was also riding back to join her and was ascending the ridge from the Alder Creek side.

Chico had mounted his horse when he saw Crossley-Hunt coming up the side of the hill. He did not intend moving unless he had to and was fairly confident that he would not be detected. But inadvertently he had moved his horse onto a small ant hill. As it felt the insects crawling up its legs, the pony snorted and bounded forward. A low branch almost swept Chico from his saddle but the branch broke with a loud crack as the horse jumped into the open.

Mary looked toward the sound in time to see a rider frantically spurring his horse back into the trees. Something told her that the stranger meant trouble and she started her pony down the slope toward the Englishman.

Chico cursed under his breath and was about to escape detection by turning his mount down the Alder Creek side of the hill when he saw Connell riding up. Hoping to avoid a gunfight he turned back the way he had come, aiming for the northern end of the range.

'Be careful, Cliff,' the girl called, as soon as the company man was close enough. 'There's someone on the ridge.'

Connell heard her warning as his mount topped the hill. 'It's only me, Mary,' he called.

'It's not you, Tom. I saw a man on a horse

further along the ridge.'

Crossley-Hunt had joined the girl by then. 'Wait here,' he ordered, as he undid the flap on his holster. 'Tom and I will have a look.'

'No point in giving him an easy shot,' Connell said. 'Let's keep wide apart and get over the open ground fast.'

Both men touched spurs to their horses and raced across the bare area toward the pine trees. Ahead they could plainly hear a horse crashing through the trees and undergrowth. The mysterious stranger was running and they wanted to know why.

Trusting to his sure-footed pony and his own riding skill, Chico reached the end of the ridge and set his mount down the steep slope. With forelegs stiff, the little roan sat back on its haunches and slid down, spraying loose rocks and gravel ahead of it. A sudden stop was impossible when the horse slid through a few young pines to find McLeod's posse directly in its path.

Coventry yelled in alarm as the roan pony crashed into his big black. The horse outweighed Chico's mount by a good 300 pounds and, though it staggered, it did not go down. Even so, the impact knocked the little rancher from his saddle and sent him rolling down the hill.

Aware that he would be caught with the incriminating rifle, Chico drew his Colt and tried to shoot his way clear of trouble. He snapped a shot at McLeod, missed, but then as he swept by, switched his aim to Raymond. But before he could squeeze the trigger, the deputy, Roberts, fired and knocked him from his saddle. He hit the ground and slid in the loose gravel, coming to rest against the trunk of a tree.

McLeod triggered two quick shots and at such short range, did not miss. Chico shuddered under the impact and Roberts fired again and he rolled forward on to his face.

'Give him another one,' Raymond urged. 'Don't let him get up.'

'No need,' the sheriff observed. 'He won't be getting up. He's good and dead.'

'Who's there?' Crossley-Hunt's voice called from higher up the hill. He had no intention of arriving at a gunfight unannounced.

'It's McLeod. Come down easy and don't make any wrong moves. There's one of your friends here – just charged us out of nowhere.'

Connell and Crossley-Hunt guided their horses down the slope to where the posse watched suspiciously. Both men recognized the roan pony.

'We were after him, 'Connell explained. 'But we didn't know it was Chico.'

'Well you know, now.' As he spoke, Roberts leaned across and dragged the rifle from the dead man's saddle scabbard. He glanced at it and then held it up for all to see. 'Look here, folks – a .45/.75 Winchester Centennial. We've got our killer.'

The ranchers stared at each other in disbelief. All believed that Chico had worked for them. Damning him for his treachery, Coventry and the sheriff gave vent to their anger but Raymond was too overcome with relief to be angry.

'We left Mary Coulter up there on the ridge,' Connell told the sheriff. 'We'll go back to her now and then let the Alder Creek ranchers know that they are not in trouble.'

'You can tell them anything you like, but heaven help any I catch rustling. Tell them that too,' McLeod snarled.

As the pair urged their mounts back up the steep ridge, Crossley-Hunt expressed the opinion that their troubles were far from over. Chico was only one part of the puzzle. Connell agreed with him.

Jensen was surprised to see the two hands he had sent with Crossley-Hunt arrive back without him. Upon questioning, the pair brought the manager up to date on what they knew. It did not please him. He would have been happier to hear that the company man had been killed in a gunfight with rustlers. Crossley-Hunt was getting closer to the secret that the manager knew would ruin him if revealed. The fabricated crisis about the rustlers had seemed an ideal diversion but that could easily unravel.

Adams had failed in his murder attempt and he would need to disassociate the ranch operations from the dead foreman. It was important that the failed attempt should be regarded as a case of personal animosity.

Jensen was now regretting that he had given the job to Adams. He should have hired Chico so that the murder had no connection to the ranch. But it was not too late. He decided to seek out the half-breed. 'Prudence!' he bellowed. 'Get in here.'

The maid almost ran into the room, nervously wiping her hands on her apron as she came. 'What is it, Mr Jensen?'

'Go over to the bunkhouse and tell the boys that I'm looking for Chico. If anyone knows where he is, I want him pronto.'

'Wouldn't he be tracking for Sheriff McLeod's posse?'

'Not according to the men who came from there. Now, get moving.'

Like a frightened mouse, Prudence scuttled away.

SEVENTEEN

'So what happens now?' Hank Coates asked, as he attacked the steak that Coulter had provided for his fellow ranchers who had gathered at his spread. After a tension-filled day, the defenders of Alder Creek could finally relax.

'With Chico dead there should be a lot less killing,' another suggested.

'If anything, Chico was on our side,' Bill Sutton reminded. 'Coventry and his friends are still around and they still reckon we're rustlers. Things for us ain't changed much at all.'

Crossley-Hunt heard the remark and disagreed. 'The Association's power has been weakened considerably. Raymond at the Double T no longer has riders and I intend to make sure that the Diamond R does not get involved in any illegal lynching.'

'That might work while you are here, Cliff,'

Coulter told him, 'but eventually you have to go home and with you out of the way, Jensen is likely to get up to his old tricks again.'

'Things might be different at the Diamond R very shortly,' the Englishman said. Then before any could ask further questions, he went looking for Connell. He found the former deputy deep in conversation with Mary Coulter. They seemed oblivious to the noisy barbecue only a few yards away. Something told him that neither would appreciate his interruption but he felt it was justified.

'Sorry to interrupt,' he said, 'but could I see you for a moment, please, Tom?'

Connell's glare would have killed a more sensitive man at fifty yards, but he excused himself and walked over to where the Englishman waited. 'This had better be important, Cliff.'

It was. Connell had found new employment.

Crossley-Hunt had hired him for sixty dollars a month to patrol the range and watch for trouble from any source. There was another task as well. He was to ride to Lodgepole and send a telegraph message that Crossley-Hunt would write to the company's lawyer in New York. The lawyer was to engage a private investigator in an attempt to track the movements of the imported bulls. From the ranch records, the company man had the name of the ship and the date that the animals were landed in New York.

'How quickly could you get to Lodgepole?' he asked Connell.

'I could be there by morning when the telegraph office opens. You write the message and I'll make sure it's sent. I might need another horse though, I have been working my own pretty hard the last few days.'

'You have to pass the Diamond R. Leave your horse and pick up one of ours. I'll give you written authorization to use a Diamond R horse in case someone thinks you are a horse-thief. But I would prefer that nobody knew about your journey.'

Connell chuckled. 'I've hunted my share of horse-thieves and have learned a trick or two along the way. Nobody at the Diamond R is going to see me take that horse tonight. Start writing that message. I'll get back to Mary now. Let me know when you are ready.'

'Sorry to tear you away,' Crossley-Hunt joked.

'You sure as hell don't look it. Don't go trying to steal her while I'm gone. You English gentlemen have a certain reputation, you know.'

'Don't worry, Tom. Nobody ever accused me of being a gentleman.'

A short while later, with Crossley-Hunt's message in his pocket, Connell set out on the first leg of his journey. The company man would return to the Diamond R later. He was in no hurry to acquaint Jensen with what had happened.

127

A light was showing in the ranch-house window when Connell quietly led his horse into the pasture where the ranch's working horses were kept. Bending low so that the animals' shapes were outlined against the night sky, he quickly found a short-backed, square-built type that he judged would suit his needs. The horse was no trouble to catch and it took only a few minutes to unsaddle and rub the chestnut's back before turning it loose. With his bridle and saddle on his new mount, he led it out of the pasture and walked until he was a safe distance from the ranch buildings. Lodgepole was thirty miles away, but he was in no hurry. He did not want to be seen around town too long before the telegraph office opened.

The night was cool and the fresh horse stepped out smartly. Because the dark-brown gelding was a good walker, the rider was able to make good progress without the risk of an accident on the rough trail.

A couple of times he halted along the way at patches of good grass and allowed his mount periods of rest and grazing. Connell was tired but was travelling light and knew there would be no rest trying to sleep on damp ground wrapped in a sweaty saddle blanket. He would find somewhere to rest for a while after he was sure that Crossley-Hunt's message was on its way.

Lodgepole was just coming to life when he rode

down the main street to the telegraph office. The operator had just opened the doors when Connell arrived. He looked at the message and carefully counted the words. 'This won't be cheap,' he announced, as he did some quick calculations on a piece of paper.

'I didn't expect it would be,' Connell replied, as he took out a couple of notes from his pants pocket. Crossley-Hunt had given him the money with the message. There was enough change to pay for a rider to deliver any reply to the Diamond R when one arrived. He made it quite plain that confidential business was involved and that any reply should go directly to Crossley-Hunt without delay.

With the main task out of the way, Connell arranged for his mount to be fed at the livery stable and sought breakfast at the closest of the town's three hotels. After he had eaten he arranged for a couple of hours' sleep in the hay loft of the livery stable.

He was not sure how long he had been asleep when he heard a familiar voice below.

'Billy, are you there?' The voice belonged to Sheriff McLeod.

Another voice, that of Roberts, said, 'He's probably down at Nielsen's arranging for more feed. We can look around here. That chestnut horse of Connell's should be easy to spot.'

'Are you sure it was Connell you saw going into the hotel?'

'Pretty sure, but maybe he left town while I was looking for you.'

'He can thank his lucky stars if he did because he's as good as dead. We can't let him say too much about the lack of a rustler problem. The Association wouldn't like it.'

'But, Monty, how do we explain it?' Roberts asked.

'That's easy. If we shoot him in town, we claim he was working for the rustlers. If we shoot him out on the range he can just be another rustlers' victim. You wait here for Billy. I'm going back to get a couple more men and then we'll turn Lodgepole upside down. If he's here we have to find him.'

Connell lay still in the loft hardly daring to make a sound. He needed to get out of Lodgepole and had only limited time. With Roberts waiting below that would not be easy. Peering over the edge of the loft, he saw the deputy below him. A couple of hay bales were nearby on the upper level and Connell suddenly saw an answer to his problem. He lifted one silently and dropped it on the man below.

The bale was soft but heavy and it knocked the big deputy to the ground. Half-stunned and totally surprised, Roberts seemed to have trouble

comprehending what was happening. The delay
gave Connell time to swing down from the loft and
plant his boot in the middle of the prostrate man's
back. Simultaneously he cocked his gun and
rammed it against the deputy's head. 'Move and
you're dead,' he growled.

Roberts was suddenly aware of his peril and
ceased all resistance. 'Don't shoot. I ain't moving.'

Connell plucked the revolver from the other's
holster. 'That's real smart of you, Jed. You won't be
hurt if you do as I say. When I tell you, get up
slowly but keep facing the back of the stable.'

The deputy did as instructed and stood with his
hands high. 'What do you want, Tom?'

'You can start by putting that bridle and saddle
on the brown horse in that stall beside you – and
keep on the near side where I can watch you.'

With little choice Roberts obeyed.

'Now bring the horse out here and lead him
around a bit. He blows out and I don't want the
saddle rolling.'

Roberts led the horse a couple of paces and
offered the reins to his captor, but Connell had no
intention of moving so close to such a dangerous
man. 'Drop the reins,' he ordered 'and move back
facing the wall.'

Juggling reins, gun and latigo, Connell tightened the cinch another few inches. When he was
satisfied, he led the horse out of the stable, but

kept his gun trained on Roberts. 'I'll shoot you if you appear in that door before I leave,' he threatened.

'I ain't moving.' The deputy was thankful to be alive and had no intention of taking any risks.

Connell mounted quickly, threw the deputy's gun in a nearby horse trough and galloped away.

McLeod alerted by the pounding of hoofs, emerged from his office to see his former deputy racing past him. He swore under his breath and called to the two rough-looking characters who had followed him out the door. 'That's Connell. Get after him.' Then, with surprising speed for a big man, he ran to his horse hitched nearby and threw himself into the saddle. His companions unhitched their own mounts and seconds later, all three were in hot pursuit.

Connell had roughly 200 yards start but actually steadied his mount's rush. He had a long way to ride and going too hard too soon would quickly exhaust his horse. He knew that he had to make his hunters ride harder than he was so their mounts would fail sooner.

Gambling that he would be very unlucky to be hit by a hard-riding shooter, he steadied the brown horse a little more. A glance over his shoulder showed that McLeod was working his spurs vigorously and was closing the gap between them. The sheriff's horse was a good one, but the combination of great weight and lung-bursting speed would soon take its toll.

Encouraged by the way his mount was overhauling his quarry, the big man plied the spurs savagely in an attempt to get into shooting range. Gradually his horse shortened the distance. The animal had thrown all its strength into the contest and now was within thirty yards of Connell's mount. The sheriff tried a shot but, predictably, it missed.

Aware of the danger from a lucky shot, Connell judged that it was time to increase his lead. 'Now, let's break their hearts,' he told the brown horse as he allowed a little more rein. The animal stretched out its neck and lengthened its stride moving easily away from the sheriff's foam-covered bay that, in response to its rider's urgings, had spent itself too soon. In seconds the bay fell back and soon McLeod's henchmen had caught up with their leader. Their horses were carrying considerably less weight but were only average quality.

'He's getting away,' the sheriff shouted, but then noted that one of his men had a Winchester on his saddle. 'Try a rifle shot,' he ordered.

The man hauled his mount to a stop, vaulted from the saddle and grabbed his carbine. Fortunately for Connell, the other two riders had not stopped as quickly and they moved between the shooter and his target.

'Get outa the way!' the rifleman called, while

running to the side to get a view around his companions. By this time Connell was 200 yards away. But a man panting from hard riding and running does not shoot well. The first shot hit so far behind the target that the rifleman realized that he had not adjusted his rear sight. With no time to make the necessary correction, he aimed high and tried again. Again the distinctive thump of a striking bullet failed to reward his efforts. Then Connell was over a low hill and out of sight.

'You're a good one,' he told the horse, patting its sweaty neck as he slowed to a trot. He had shaken off the pursuit but it was still a long way to the Diamond R.

McLeod knew that he was beaten temporarily but refused to admit defeat. 'I know where he's going,' he told the others. 'He's going to the Diamond R, then possibly Alder Creek. We're not far from Coventry's ranch. We'll go there and I'll swear in the Wineglass crew as deputies. Coventry will give us fresh horses. Connell and his friend Crossways are in for a surprise. This time I'm not worrying about the niceties of the law. We can shoot hell out of that pair first and then work out a suitable story later. Then we can clear out that rats' nest along Alder Creek. The time for pussy-footing around is over.'

EIGHTEEN

An air of tension hung over the ranch house at the Diamond R. Raymond was still with them as he feared to go back to the all but deserted Double T. He knew that Chico was dead, but suspected that someone else had hired him. The half-breed had been a hired gun and he suspected that his men had been killed on the instructions of someone from Alder Creek. His men had participated in the lynching of John Murphy and although he had not been present, Raymond had authorized his crew to take the action that they did.

Jensen was short-tempered and anxious. He had seen Crossley-Hunt poring over the ranch books and was fearful that he might find how he had padded some of the bills and siphoned off a considerable sum of money. Over the years Regency Estates had not queried the temporary employment of the occasional fictitious cowhand,

135

but their representative was starting to ask questions and could find out that the non-existent hands had been hired at a time when ranch work was fairly slack. The deal with the bulls had looked easy at the time. Through a crooked livestock agent, he had sold the Black Angus bulls not long after they arrived in the East and they had brought a good price. Then the conspirators had bought cheap, cross-bred animals from an eastern farm, had them suitably branded and sent them West after splitting the profits between themselves. Most westerners had never seen a Black Angus and were unlikely to know that a substitution had taken place. If Crossley-Hunt checked with Loeb Livestock on his way back East, there was a good chance that the fraud would be discovered.

The company man had his own worries. He did not believe that Adams had acted independently when he made the attempt on his life. So far he had fallen out with the Cattlemen's Association, the sheriff and quite a few ranch hands. Jensen was pretending to be friendly, but was hardly convincing. Crossley-Hunt preferred his enemies to come from the front but doubted that they would in this case.

There had been a few awkward moments when a cowhand reported the presence of a strange horse in the remuda and that a good one from the late foreman's string was missing. The company man explained that he had hired someone to send an important telegraph message.

Jensen and Raymond knew immediately who owned the chestnut horse and did not hesitate to ask why such action was necessary. The manager also asked what was so important that it could not wait until regular hours.

The time for diplomacy was past and Crossley-Hunt told them straight, 'I felt that I could not trust any of our hands,' he said. 'They might be loyal to you, but that does not mean that they are loyal to the company. The contents of that message were highly confidential and I needed a man I could trust.'

'And you don't trust your own men?' Jensen accused.

'Not with the company they've been keeping.'

'And that includes me?'

'You're damn right it does. A lot of strange things have been going on around here. You might think that murder is a normal part of beef production, but I do not. I'm on the verge of firing you, Jensen, so feel free to resign if you consider that you are being unjustly treated.'

The manager flushed angrily and was about to reply when Prudence appeared at the door. 'Tom Connell's back,' she announced before disappearing again.

Crossley-Hunt strode outside in time to see

Connell dismounting. 'I sent your message,' the latter told him. 'But trouble could be following me. McLeod and Roberts tried to kill me. They're really after my hide. If they get fresh horses they could turn up here.'

'Stand right where you are – the pair of you.'

Jensen's voice was accompanied by the sound of a gun being cocked.

The pair turned to see the manager glaring at them over the sights of a Colt .45. Behind him, Raymond was also belatedly drawing his gun. With a crooked smile on his lips, Jensen told them, 'That's right handy to know you're wanted by the law, Connell. Nobody's gonna doubt that you showed up here and killed poor Mr Crossways-Hunt.'

'You won't get away with this.' Connell was playing for time. He had to keep the other man talking, hoping that his concentration would lapse and he would have half a chance to go for his own gun.

The company man guessed what he was planning and he too attempted to create a diversion. 'He's right, Jensen. You can't cover up a double murder.'

'Can't I? Too bad you won't be around to see how it's—'

The 20-gauge shotgun sounded like a cannon. It was a light weapon loaded with bird shot that the ranch cook used to keep the hawks away from their chickens,but the tiny pellets hit Jensen and knocked him sideways. A few also struck Raymond and the gun he had just drawn fell from a wounded hand.

Connell's gun was out in a split second and he fired at Jensen as he struggled to rise. The manager fell back as the bullet entered at the base of his neck and tore its way down into his chest. But somehow he retained his grasp on the gun so Connell fired again before switching his attention to Raymond. But he need not have worried.

Crossley-Hunt already had his gun in the wounded rancher's face and was coolly telling him how he would relish the opportunity to shoot him.

Prudence snapped open her shotgun and replaced the spent cartridges. There was even a rare smile on her face.

'You saved us, Prudence,' the company man said. 'Thank you for your unexpected but very timely intervention.'

'It was a pleasure,' the small woman said and meant it. 'Too bad I didn't put a few more pellets into Raymond while I was at it.'

'I'm badly wounded,' the injured man groaned. 'I need medical help.' Then he turned to the woman. 'Prudence, why did you shoot us?'

'I shot you because you murdered my nephew, John Murphy. I was such a nobody around here that no one knew that my maiden name was Murphy. Nobody took any notice of me and, day after day, I heard you and your friends plotting and scheming. You thought nothing of murder. I even heard you and the others discussing John's killing. I wrote down the names, but then I realized that I couldn't go to the law because the law was as crooked as you are. Finally I gave the names to John's son, Chico. John's wife, who died years before you came here, was a Shoshone. Chico was their child. He was christened Charles Murphy but spent most of his life in Texas. You people thought Chico was working for you, but he was working for the Murphy clan.'

'But I had no part in lynching Murphy,' Raymond protested. 'I wasn't there.'

The submissive voice was gone and Prudence spoke angrily. 'You sent your men to do it. I heard the plans that you and the others made right in this ranch house. Coventry's men murdered Martel and your turn came next. The idea was that each of the three ranches should lynch one small rancher so that all would be implicated. Mr Crossley-Hunt's visit stopped Jensen from taking his turn.'

The company man interrupted. 'Then it was you, Prudence, who left the note warning that Tom was in danger?'

'That's right, but he had nothing to fear from

140

Chico; it was the men who were plotting to have him killed.'

'I'm bleeding,' Raymond whined.

'That's good,' Prudence snapped. 'I hope it's painful.'

'It might be an idea to get Raymond out of here,' Connell suggested. 'McLeod could be here soon. Let's patch up his arm and get him to Alder Creek where he can answer a few questions in front of witnesses.'

Though Raymond was horrified at the prospect, Crossley-Hunt liked that idea and he and Prudence tended to their prisoner's wounds while Connell saddled the horses. Raymond by then was in a state of sheer terror at the thought of being taken to Alder Creek and it suited his captors to let him think that he would possibly share the same fate as the alleged rustlers.

The ranch hands had been out on the range and would not have heard the shooting but George, the crippled handyman, and the cook certainly had. The old cowboy came hobbling from one of the sheds and his eyes widened in surprise to see Jensen sprawled on the ground. 'What happened?'

'Jensen tried to kill me,' the company man said smoothly. He thought it best not to mention Prudence's part in the shooting. 'I had to take a shotgun to him. Unfortunately Mr Raymond took sides but chose the wrong one. Connell and I are taking him to be patched up.'

'They ain't,' Raymond cried. 'Don't believe him. They're taking me to Alder Creek. They're gonna lynch me.'

Gus Lawler, the cook, took his shotgun back from Prudence, stared blankly at the scene for a second and muttered to George, 'We didn't see any of this, did we?'

'Not a dad-blamed thing,' the old man agreed. Together they walked back indoors. Neither held the members of the Cattlemen's Association in much esteem and had been secretly pleased by the sudden turn of events.

As Connell led up the horses, Crossley-Hunt said to Prudence, 'If McLeod comes calling, blame the shooting on me and don't try to conceal where we went. This will all be sorted out legally later, but Regency Estates will look after any legal problems you might have. Raymond won't come to any harm from us unless he does something stupid.'

'As long as that murdering weasel gets what's coming to him, I don't care how it happens,' the maid said emphatically. 'You'd better get going,' she said. 'I can see a big cloud of dust over there on the trail. Looks like McLeod's not too far away.'

Aware that help could be near at hand, Raymond started to struggle again until Connell threatened to knock him unconscious with a gun butt and tie him on a horse. Reluctantly the captive mounted his horse.

Crossley-Hunt ran back into the office and reappeared with a Winchester and a box of ammunition. 'We might need these,' he said, as he mounted.

'We'll need them sooner than you think, if we don't get moving,' Connell reminded him. Then, as the trio turned their mounts for Alder Creek, he told Raymond, 'Don't try any tricks. This horse of mine will catch yours in two jumps if you try to get away and I'll blow you out of the saddle. This is the only warning you're getting.'

The rancher knew he was not joking and quickly put spurs to his mount fearful of being left behind. As they went out the back gate of the ranch, McLeod, Coventry and a dozen men were reining in their horses at the Diamond R ranch house.

NINETEEN

The posse halted only briefly at the Diamond R. As instructed, Prudence told the sheriff that Jensen had been killed in a gunfight with Crossley-Hunt and Connell. When he heard that they were only minutes behind the pair and that Raymond had been taken prisoner, the sheriff was secretly pleased.

As he led his party away, he said quietly to Coventry, 'This is perfect. If we kill Raymond, we can blame it on the others. Of course, we have to kill them too, because Connell knows about the herd our joint venture is bringing in and even if he hasn't told Crossways, we need him out of the way as well. We can always blame his death on a deputy who went bad, namely Connell. The English owners of the Diamond R are too far away to really know what's going on. Before today's out, if we play our cards right, we'll have the Double T and the Diamond R right out of the game and the small ranchers well and truly on the run. Jack, old pard, this is working out better than I had hoped.'

'Don't get too excited, Monty. We need to kill at least three people first and they have a start on us. If they get to Alder Creek, we could have trouble.'

'I've thought of that. Roberts and a couple of others are already selecting fresh horses from here. They'll ride them to death if necessary to get close enough to pick off our men. Roberts has that long-range rifle of Chico's and he's a good shot.'

The posse had scarcely travelled a mile when the deputy and two others overtook them on fresh horses and soon left them behind.

Raymond was giving trouble. He deliberately slowed his horse and rode it on the roughest ground that he could, anything to delay his arrival at Alder Creek. Once the animal stumbled and he deliberately fell off.

Connell called the dismounted rancher a few uncomplimentary names as he caught the loose horse.

'I've busted something,' Raymond wailed. 'My arm hurts and I think I might have broken my shoulder. I can't ride.'

'Who cares?' Connell growled. 'I'm happy enough to throw you over the saddle and tie you there. Now get on that horse.'

'Be quick about it,' Crossley-Hunt said, as he

pointed behind them.

Three hard-riding horsemen had come into view. Even as the others watched, the foremost rider reined in his mount and jumped from the saddle hauling free a rifle as he went. A second later he was prone on the ground and selecting a target. The first shot hit Raymond's horse before the sound of the rifle carried to them. The animal staggered, grunted and went down. Another bullet whined off a rock beside the Englishman.

Connell acted quickly. He removed the lariat from his saddle and flipped a loop around their prisoner's neck. He passed the other end of the rope to Crossley-Hunt. 'If he tries to get away, drag him to death.' After removing his carbine from the saddle, he ordered Raymond, 'Get on my horse and do as Cliff says, or you're going to get killed.'

Another bullet kicked up dust at Connell's feet as he loaded the protesting rancher onto the chestnut horse. The company man took up the slack of the rope and wound it around his saddle horn. 'What are you planning, Tom?'

'There's a nice little nest of rocks over there. I'm going to hole up for a while. You get this coyote over to Alder Creek and bring back a bit of help. I could need it when the rest of that posse shows up. Now get going.'

Reluctantly, Crossley-Hunt urged his horse up the range towing a very frightened prisoner behind him. The move caught the distant rifleman by surprise as he had not expected the party to split up. He wasted one shot at Connell and by that time the two riders were lost to sight among the pines on the hillside.

Connell paused long enough to put a bullet into the head of the wounded horse and then sprinted across fifty yards of open ground to the position he had selected in the rocks.

Roberts could not fire as rapidly as he would have liked because a lever-action rifle is difficult to reload when flat on the ground. Finally he decided to waste no more ammunition. 'We stopped one of them,' he told his companions.

The lanky man beside him observed the scene for a second and said in a worried tone, 'That *hombre* might also be able to stop us. From where he is, his Winchester can reach anyone trying to go over that hill behind him. It could cost us men to try getting into Alder Creek that way. McLeod ain't gonna be real impressed with this situation.'

'Don't worry about McLeod,' Roberts muttered. 'I'll keep this cuss's head down. You pair work forward on foot till you get in good range for your carbines. We might still be able to clear the way before the posse comes up.'

Seconds later, long-range shots were striking the rocks that sheltered Connell and whining off into the distance. Roberts had the range judged

147

perfectly and his target could only stay under cover and hope that a stray shot did not find its way between the rocks.

Peering through a narrow space where two boulders came together. Connell saw two men with rifles bent low and running from one piece of cover to the other. It would not take them long to reach a point where they were in effective range for their repeaters. He had miscalculated badly, expecting all to move into carbine range offering him shots without himself being pinned down by a more powerful weapon. He would need to alter his tactics if he hoped to survive. Ignoring the covering fire, Connell crawled around to where he could see the approaching riflemen through a thin screen of weeds that offered concealment but no protection.

At 200 yards the posse men halted and tried a few shots. A couple struck the boulders and others raised spurts of dust just in front of them.

Connell did not return the fire.

Confident that the deputy's rifle was pinning their intended victim down, the pair grew bolder and now made longer rushes before going to ground again. The lanky rifleman was in easy range and thinking himself unobserved was becoming careless.

Connell settled his sights on the front of the man's checkered shirt and squeezed the trigger.

The bullet hit the target dead centre punching him backwards and sending his rifle flying from his grasp. The untidy tangle of immobile limbs on the ground was a certain indication that the rifleman was dead. His companion reacted quickly and sent a bullet into the weeds where gunsmoke had betrayed Connell's position. The latter rolled back behind the rocks his face stinging from a shower of gravel that the bullet had kicked up.

The attacker took no further risks, going to ground behind a large log. From there he could fire without risking the open ground between himself and the former deputy.

A glance around the other side of his rocky barrier showed Connell that the main body of the posse had now arrived. The odds against him had increased from daunting to almost impossible.

Coventry made sure he was well out of rifle range where he halted his big, black horse. He took in the scene and turned to McLeod who had been talking to Roberts. 'What are they waiting for?' he demanded angrily. 'There are enough of us to charge him. He wouldn't stand a chance.'

'That's right; he wouldn't, but sure as hell there would be some dead men, maybe three or four. My guess is that it's Connell over there and he's known to shoot pretty well. Feel free to lead any charge you want, Jack, but I don't reckon too many will follow you. Out in front on that big horse you would likely be the first to get hit, but if you're so all-fired keen to go, I won't stop you.'

Suddenly the little rancher had second thoughts. 'How would you handle it?'

'I'd send a couple of men wide to work around him and get onto the high ground. They might be able to shoot down on Connell and, at the same time, pick off any help coming over the ridge from Alder Creek.'

'It could work,' Coventry grudgingly conceded, as though the sheriff needed his approval.

Connell noted the increase in fire and could see a couple of men keeping at long range and working up the hill to his left. Where were the Alder Creek men? It would not be long before he was under fire from three sides. If help did not arrive soon it would be too late. What had delayed the other ranchers? Crossley-Hunt had been sure that he could gain their support, but it seemed that he might have been wrong.

TWENTY

Connell was sparing with his ammunition and only fired when one of the other side became careless and remained exposed for too long. He thought he might have wounded another man but could not be sure. For every shot he fired, a dozen came back. They knocked chips off the boulders and those that struck the ground near him raised spurts of gravel that stung exposed parts of his body. He was pushing cartridges through the Winchester's loading gate when a bullet plucked at the leg of his pants. As he hastily withdrew the limb, Connell knew that a rifleman had worked around his left flank where there was less protection. He was gradually being forced into a more cramped position. It was only a matter of time before a bullet from this new direction struck him somewhere.

Thrusting his rifle around the side of a boulder,

he saw the head and shoulders of the shooter showing above a rock. The man was sighting his rifle and was about to shoot. Even as Connell's finger tightened on the trigger he saw his target lurch sideways and disappear from view. He was vaguely conscious of a rifle report from the hill behind him. Hope returned. Initially he thought that the Alder Creek ranchers had arrived and someone was keeping the posse members away from his most vulnerable side. But the hope dwindled quickly when he realized that it was only one man. His first thought was that Crossley-Hunt had been unable to enlist any support and had returned to give what assistance he could. Determined not to give his enemies an easy victory, he snapped another shot at a posse member who was trying to work closer. The bullet missed but the target fled back to more adequate shelter.

Another couple of men were working their way into a place that would enable them to cover both Connell's position and the bare crest of the hill over which any Alder Creek reinforcements would most likely come. Connell's hidden ally targeted these men and sent them diving for cover Unfortunately a cloud of gunsmoke betrayed the shooter's position.

McLeod swore and pointed. 'Connell's got help. I'll bet that's Crossways come back to help him. He mustn't have been able to get the Alder Creek crowd to join him. This is great. We have the pair of them now.'

'We've lost a couple of men,' Roberts reminded his boss. 'Those two are well under cover. I reckon we'll lose a few more trying to pry them out.'

'Not necessarily. Those characters might not be carrying much ammunition and neither can get any water. After another hour in the sun, who knows if they will still have any fight left in them. Time's on our side because if the Alder Creek crowd had intended taking a hand they would have been riding over that ridge by now and we have some men over there who could cut them up pretty fierce if they did show up. If our side fires enough shots at the other pair we'll get lucky sooner or later.'

Coventry was clearly frustrated by the situation. He paced about with a rifle in his hands but made no effort to move up to the firing line. 'How much longer can they hold out?' he asked the sheriff.

'Not a great deal longer,' McLeod told him. 'You'll notice that they ain't shooting back quite so often now. My guess is that they are running low on rifle ammunition. Once they run out we can move closer and really settle their hash.'

Connell had reached the same conclusion. He fed his last five rounds into the rifle and drew his Colt. Though it lacked the range and the accuracy of the rifle, the bullets would carry a considerable distance if given sufficient elevation. He would save the rifle until he had sure targets. Both to experiment and to discourage the others from rushing his position, he aimed high and fired a shot at a boulder that he knew was sheltering a posse member. Dust flew near the base of the rock and he knew that he would have to aim higher.

Roberts was quick to note the difference in the reports. 'That wasn't a Winchester he just fired. I think Connell is out of rifle ammo. We can move our men a bit closer to him now. Long-range shooting with a sixgun is not very dangerous.'

'Move up!' McLeod shouted to his scattered men. 'But keep out of sixgun range.'

Connell could see the cordon tightening around him but was loath to fire his remaining rifle shots. The rifleman covering him was a hundred yards further back and the support would end when he ran out of rifle cartridges. His companion might yet escape, but Connell had too many guns too close to him. He would have to fight to the last.

Then, he heard the horses. But they were not coming from the direction of Alder Creek.

A group of riders on foam-covered horses came sweeping around the base of the hill and straight into the rear of the posse. The tall figure of Crossley-Hunt was noticeable among the foremost horsemen.

Coventry had turned upon hearing the hoof-beats and then yelled in alarm as the newcomers bore down on them. Roberts wheeled about and fired a hasty shot. He hit a horse but the animal did not go down immediately and its long, lurching run carried it almost to the deputy. Even as he reloaded, a shotgun blast fired by the rider, cut Roberts down. The attack was so unexpected that the posse men had no time to regroup or offer any co-ordinated resistance. Panic set in. Connell was forgotten and most ran for where they had left their horses.

Connell stood erect and emptied his rifle into the fleeing men. He saw one fall before his ammunition was expended. Drawing his Colt, he sought another target but there was none in range.

Crossley-Hunt came out of his saddle and hit the ground running, his eyes fixed on the bulky form of McLeod. The Adams revolver, yet unfired was clasped in his right hand. He was in no mood to worry about prisoners.

The sheriff saw him coming and snapped a quick shot in the company-man's direction. The Englishman ignored the hastily aimed bullet and fired two quick, double-action shots. Both took effect. McLeod staggered but was still on his feet and raising his revolver for another shot.

'Drop it, McLeod.' The warning was quite clear.

'Go to hell, Crossways,' the big man snarled, as

he struggled to sight his weapon.

One of the nearby Alder Creek ranchers settled the matter. He fired a rifle bullet into the sheriff's heart. 'Serves you right, you big, ugly sonofabitch,' the man shouted, before turning to seek other targets.

Coventry managed to get through the confusion of wheeling horses, swirling dust and men shouting and shooting. He unhitched the reins of his terrified horse but the animal was in a blind panic and sought to pull away from him. As he struggled with it he realized that he could not reach the stirrup. Seizing the saddle horn he attempted to vault into the saddle but again was defeated by the animal's height and its violent attempts to run off.

He was still clinging to the saddle when Ben Coulter rode up close and shot him through the head. 'You won't murder any more ranchers,' he muttered.

Almost as quickly as it started, the battle stopped. The surviving posse members were standing there with raised hands and hoping that the blood lust of the Alder Creek men had been satisfied.

Connell looked about puzzled. If it had not been Crossley-Hunt backing him up, who was it? He turned and in amazement saw Mary Coulter, rifle in hand, carefully picking her way down the rough hillside. He ran to meet her. 'Mary, you saved my life. Thank you for that. Things were rather grim there for a while. But how did you get there?'

The girl laughed. 'Glad I could help. I was keeping watch up on the hill. I saw you were in trouble and decided to help out. It was lucky that I got here in time.'

Crossley-Hunt, leading his horse and reloading the Adams as he came, strolled across to the pair.

'You sure took your time,' Connell said in mock anger.

'Sorry, but I had no intention of leading our men into an ambush. McLeod was expecting us to come over the hill so we took the long way round the hill and came in behind them. We have some very tired horses but no serious casualties. With their leaders gone the rest of our opponents see no reason to fight. I think that the war is over now.'

Connell shook his head doubtfully. 'There are a million loose ends here.'

Crossley-Hunt laughed. 'That's why Regency Estates employs lawyers. They'll get things sorted out. What are you going to do now?'

'I'm going to get one of the posse horses and escort Mary home. Her mother must be having a fit. Then I'll pick up my own horses from Coulters'.'

'When you do that, call back to the Diamond R;

I have a proposition for you. Now, I'd better get back to helping here. I think I can say on behalf of the ranchers here that we owe both of you a vote of thanks.'

EPILOGUE

Crossley-Hunt's proposition was that Connell should take over management of the Diamond R, a position that he gladly accepted. The weeks following the battle had been hectic. The ranchers had formed a new association with all included. One of its first acts was to send a delegation to turn back the herd that Coventry's son was bringing into the area. Aware of his father's fate, the son was only too happy to sell the herd and see them shipped East. In anticipation of a severe winter, Connell also set about culling the Diamond R herd. Old stock and barren cows would be driven to the railhead for sale rather than have them die later after taking grass that was needed by the better animals.

Enquiries resulting from Crossley-Hunt's telegraph message confirmed that Jensen had illegally sold the pure-bred Black Angus bulls and pocketed the proceeds of the substitution. The ranch had lost on that deal, but the company man would recommend more imports.

Joe Raymond, after signing a confession, had been allowed to 'escape' and was last seen on a stolen but very poor quality horse heading for Mexico.

'There's only one thing worrying me,' Crossley-Hunt told Connell, at the railroad depot just before he boarded the train for his homeward journey. 'I have noticed the ranch horses being worn down of late and a beaten path being worn between the Diamond R and the Coulter place. It might save time and horseflesh if you married that girl. When I come back here in three years' time, I'll expect to see at least one child named after me.'

'Who in the hell would call a kid Crosscut?' Connell joked.

'Now don't you start—'